LOST IN THE HIGHLANDS

The Thirteen Scotsman

A SCOTTISH TIME TRAVEL ROMANCE

LORRAINE BEAUMONT

Edenbrooke Hollow Series

We Three Witches- *A Good Spell Gone Wrong*

We Three Witches – Book Two Coming Soon

New Series in the works

For all the Lasses

GRANDFATHER MOUTAIN,
NORTH CAROLINA, PRESENT DAY

Smoothing my hand over the front of my plaid, I stepped out of the changing room and spun around for my audience of one.

"Paige, aren't ye a bonny looking lass, wearing that plaid as if it were yer verra own." Tavner let out a low appreciative whistle. He was one of the original council members for the Highland Games here on Grandfather Mountain.

"Tavner, you're gonna make me blush."

"Aye, I like ta do more than that if only I was a wee bit younger," he winked.

"Oh, stop." My face heated.

"Now get on with ye, lass, and get yer reading done before the line gets too long."

"Why do I need a reading?"

"It's a custom since ye are a virgin,"

"What?" My eyes boggled.

"Ah, not that kind of virgin, lass," he chuckled and his beard quivered. "It just means ye are new to the games. The gypsy will tell ye which clan ta give yer favors ta in the games."

"What's the difference? Can't I just give them to who I want?"

"Nay, lass, that is no how it works."

"That's ridiculous. It's only a game."

Tavner's expression turned grim as he made the sign of the cross over his barrel chest. "Och lass, it is more than a game to us Scotsman."

8

"Well, of course," I tried to recant. "I didn't mean anything by it." The last thing I wanted to do was insult him.

A strange look crossed his face and then he stepped up to me. "It's all right, lass. Mistakes happen all the time." He smiled, but it didn't reach his eyes.

"So, um, where's this fortune teller's tent I need to visit?"

"Ye will no have a problem finding it. It will be the one with a line of lasses like ye waiting outside of it."

"Don't you think there should be more than one? I mean, if she is that popular."

"Only a true wanderer can give ye a reading, and she is the only one *here* that I know of."

"All righty then," I sighed and swiped a piece of my hair back from my face. "I guess I will go and get this reading done. I don't want to make another highland faux pas."

"Ye will be fine, lass. Stop off and get yerself some mead on yer way down."

"What's mead?"

"It's a drink made from fermented honey. Ye will like it."

"Thanks, Tavner."

"No, I thank ye, lass."

Several brightly striped tents were set up on the lower plateau of the mountain. After I got myself a large mug of mead, I made my way to the fortuneteller's tent; Tavner was right. There was a very long line of girls waiting outside the boldly striped tent. Sipping my mead, I stepped to the back of the line and waited my turn.

An hour later, a flock of giggling girls ran out from the tent waving banners of different colors of what clan they would represent in the games. "At this rate there won't be any clans left for me," I grumbled and took another large bite of my turkey leg.

The burly Scotsman that had been giving me strange looks off and on as I waited in line leveled his eyes on me. "Morag will see ye now." He pushed back the tent flap.

I tossed my empty cup and turkey leg bone into the trash and ducked under his arm into the dim interior.

"Come in, lass," said a crackling disembodied voice. "Have a seat and give me yer hand, lass."

The ancient woman stared straight ahead. I felt like she was looking past me at someone behind me. She was blind, or almost. After I sat down, I reached out and gave her my hand.

"It's a deal then?" The gypsy stuck out her gnarled age-spotted hand for me to shake, once we were standing outside of the tent.

"Yes. We have a deal." Afraid I might hurt her, I grabbed her hand gently. She seemed so frail all stooped over, bracing herself on her cane.

Her fingers tightened around mine until the point it was becoming painful. Tugging on my hand, I tried to get her to release mine but she was surprisingly strong.

With one last finger-crushing squeeze, she looked deeply into my eyes. "Are ye sure yer up to the task, lass?"

"Yes. I'm sure." What did she want me to do, write it in blood or something?

On cue, I felt a prick on my third finger.

"Ow". I yanked my hand.

"Not so fast, little lassie." With a surprisingly amount of nimbleness the woman pulled out an aged piece of parchment and smeared the blood from my third finger on the bottom.

"Now lass, take this pen and sign yer name here." She was overly excited; her breath was coming out in rushed hitches as she pointed to the bottom edge of the paper.

My fingers were going numb.

Just to pacify the woman, I played along. "Sure." I jerked on my hand, again, second-guessing my drunken impromptu agreement.

"Not so fast little lassie, not til ye sign," she said as though she knew what I was thinking.

"Why can't I?"

"Do ye want a Highlander for yer verra own or no?" She hitched up her brow and it disappeared under the patterned scarf tied around the top of her head.

"Fine." I took the pen from her outstretched hand and signed my name to the bottom.

The gypsy released my hand. Cackling merrily, she broke into a little jig, dancing in circles around me. Arms flapping, shuffling her feet, the stacks of bracelets on her arms made a jangling sound. She lifted her skirts and swung them back and forth. Without missing a beat, she hooked her arm through mine; then whirled me back and forth in each direction before she started a little do-si-doe move on her own.

It was the most bizarre thing I had ever seen. Before I signed the paper, the woman looked like she was going to keel over at any moment, not now though. Now she was as spry as ever, which made me wonder as to why she would act in such a way.

Unfortunately, I didn't have the chance to ponder that question for very long because when she stopped dancing, she rounded on me. Hands placed on her hips, she walked circles around where I stood, like she was sizing me up for something.

"Good, good." She patted my body affectionately, which kind-of felt more like a frisking at a police station.

"Yer a plump one, aren't ye lass?" She smacked my behind with a surprisingly amount of force, pitching me forward.

Rubbing my bottom, I frowned down at her. She reminded me of the wicked witch from Hansel & Gretel, and I was the unwitting victim about to be tossed in the oven for her dinner.

"So what of it?" I asked feeling riled.

"Oh, not ta worry." She waved her hand dismissively in the air. "Strapping Highlanders like their woman folk wit a bit o' flesh on them. So ye will do jes fine." She smiled widely, which revealed another empty space in her mouth. I had seen four spaces so far, giving more credence to the witchy character I had envisioned her as being.

Teetering on my feet, I grabbed the maypole that was set up off to the side of one of the vast open fields where the games were held. All the young pretty girls/maidens I had seen earlier were now long gone having been picked off one by one by a slew of young handsome admirers. I wasn't allowed to participate. Tavner said I picked the colors for the '13' and in doing so sealed my own fate. Whatever that was supposed to mean — so as a conciliatory prize I got myself another cup of mead. Tavner told me the drink was made from fermented honey. What he didn't tell me was how good it would taste. So one cup had turned to two, then two turned to three and the rest of the evening had become a blur and now, somehow, I ended up here, with this wicked witch, err, gypsy.

"Come on, lass, the light is waning." The gypsy grabbed my hand none too gently and led me, which was more of a dragging, across the flat of the hill over uneven clumps of grass to the base of a rather imposing mountain.

"Do ye see the steps there, lass?" She pointed her gnarled finger to the stone steps cut into the face of the mountain leading up into a bank of clouds at the top. I felt like Jack, from 'Jack and the beanstalk' as he made way to climb the great beanstalk to steal the golden egg from the Giant living in the castle in the sky.

"Uh…" I hiccupped and my vision blurred.

"Lass, can ye manage it or no?" She sounded mad, or was that fright I heard in her crackling voice as she leveled her rheumy blue-green gaze on me.

Apparently irritated with my slow response, the gypsy grabbed my arm and shook it, making my head rattle on my shoulders. "Yes, yes, I can manage it." I really wasn't too sure but I would have said anything to get away from the woman.

I wobbled forward.

"Och, lass," she screeched. "Don't go leaving the basket behind."

"What?"

"Take it, lass." She shoved a rather hefty basket into my hands. Once she let go the weight nearly made me fall on my face. I staggered back and pulled the heavy basket up.

"Take the basket of offerings, lass, to the top of the mountain, cross over the screaming bridge to the other side and the Highlander ye seek will come fer ye."

"Screaming bridge?"

"Och lass, never ye mind. Jes do as I say and all will work out for ye."

I struggled to keep hold of the basket. What in the heck was in this thing, rocks? I was about to ask her but she spoke before I could say anything.

"Now get on with ye." She shoved my bottom hard, propelling me forward.

"Best of luck ta ye, lass," she cackled and then I could swear I heard her say, "Yer going ta need it."

One by one, I took the stairs up the steep face of the mountain with my basket of bounty firmly grasped in my hands. Breathing heavily, I finally made it to the top of the mountain. The heavy wool plaid skirt was weighing me down considerably as was the basket.

Why on Earth I had to carry the basket up here was beyond me. But then again, that was the least weird thing I was doing. Climbing a mountain dressed in full Scottish clothing and carrying a basket so a Highlander would come for me out of the mist was pretty out there. But I was so drunk. Well I was, and at the time, it seemed like a perfectly sensible thing to do. Now however, as I looked around into nothing but sky, I wasn't so sure.

There was a bridge in front of me spanning a chasm of eighty or so feet and it was screaming. At least that is what it sounded like as the swinging cabled bridge shuddered in the howling wind. Gripping my basket, I stepped tentatively on the moving monstrosity, second- guessing my decision the entire time.

Taking a deep breath, I sprinted across it.

Once I was safely on the other side, I set the basket down. The wind whipped against me as I walked over to the edge of the flat rock and glanced down.

Approximately 300 feet below me were the tops of several trees. There was nothing between me and the trees except for the rock under my feet that didn't seem nearly as large as it had moments before and the sky above me. Feeling woozy, I backed up quite a bit and sat down near one of the only trees remaining on top of this desolate mountain. It wasn't much taller than me sitting down. The limbs were all twisted at awkward angles, like it was confused as to which way to grow.

The temperature was much cooler up here. I pulled my plaid more firmly around my shoulders to buffer the frigid wind.

Huddled closely to the tree, I tucked my feet under my gown, rested my elbow on my leg, and propped my chin up with my hand. Twilight was waning and the moon was drifting higher in the sky. I needed to rest a moment and then would make the long trek back down the mountain before it got too dark.

That was the plan, but the thin air from the altitude combined with my over indulgence of mead, not to mention my arduous climb up several hundred stairs, and the horror from crossing that damn bridge, made me drowsy. I decided a quick rest to revive myself wasn't such a bad idea and closed my eyes.

A shuddering underneath my bottom woke me. Disoriented, I looked around. A full moon bore down upon the mountaintop, illuminating the area in its ethereal glow as thousands of stars twinkled like diamonds just out of my reach. Again I felt the shuddering that woke me. I stumbled upward to standing as the slight shuddering turned quickly to thundering. Gripping hold of the bedraggled tree, I held on for dear life as the entire mountain shook with such force I thought for sure the damn thing was collapsing underneath me.

The thundering grew louder.

White mist swirled out towards me from the screaming bridge.

Not able to move, I watched.

One by one, horses rolled out from the mist and surrounded me. By my count, there were thirteen horses, and as my gaze lifted higher, thirteen massive Highlanders came into focus mounted on top of each one.

When the darkness came for me, I went willingly.

CHAPTER ONE

LOCH MORAR, SCOTLAND
Sometime in the reign of King James

Thirteen somber faced men wearing kilts had me surrounded and not one of them was wearing underwear.

Blinking against the bright morning light, I swallowed hard, wondering if I was dreaming. It seemed like it should be a dream since I had never seen so many fine men gathered in one place that wasn't a gay bar, and I was lying on my back staring stupidly up at them....except, I wasn't in my bed.

A man to my left grunted and nudged my leg with the toe of his boot.

"Think ye, she is dead?" asked Callum, stroking his chin. He barely began growing hair on his face and tended to massage the area in hopes it would grow faster.

"Are ye sure it's a lass?" asked Muir, who stood a full head taller than Callum and had no such desires to have a beard since it would cover his handsome visage, or so he said often. "I have never seen a lass looking like that."

"Sure, it is," said Callum, who was ten and seven and the current lairds third cousin removed. "Look at her long hair."

Muir snorted. "Callum, yer hair is down yer back and I wouldn't mistake ye for a lass, even if the night was pitched in Dragoon's blood and yer kilt was up exposing only yer hairless buttocks."

"Ye keep talking like that Muir and I may think ye want ta see me hairless buttocks more often." He lifted his aforementioned kilt and bared his backside.

"Why ye...."

The group laughed; it was a loud boisterous sound, causing splinters of pain to shoot through my head.

This exchange should have been the first clue I was somewhere I should not be. But as with most days, before I had my morning cup of lead my brain was not firing on all cylinders.

Gavin de Grey, the current laird of Greystone Castle, located on the northwest shore of Loch Morar, stepped forward. The wind whipped his dark brown hair away from his rugged profile. His blue-green gaze drifted to the bog of mud that surrounded the person his men were having a debate over. He wasn't sure if it was a lass, either. They took her from the mist and sometimes, most times, it was a lass, but every once in a while they were stuck with a man. He wasn't keen on the men. But some could cook and the others were good at mucking the stalls. Some however, ran off in the middle of the night and he had yet to find them, but then again, he wasn't looking very hard either.

If indeed this was a lass, the mud had her covered well and good, obscuring any visible clue. All he could make out was the whites of the eyes. Even the disembodied head that was the only visible part of the body gave no clue if it was a man or woman, friend or foe. Lifting his hand, he pinched the bridge of his nose, to ward off the pressure gathering between his brows.

"Do ye think she is daft?" Callum spoke from under the hand he was using to cover his mouth and nose from the smell.

"Does she look daft to ye?" Muir said, doing the same.

"She *is* lying in a filthy pit of mud," Callum noted. "Do ye ken if daft people like mud?"

"Och, how am I supposed to know?" Muir took a step back when the wind shifted.

"I can't say I've met a lass that was daft before," Callum mused.

"What about the old toothless crone ye were begging to suck yer wee bit last night?" Muir laughed.

"Och, ye promised ye wouldn't say anything about that." Callum launched himself at Muir and tackled him to the ground.

The sound of flesh hitting flesh resounded in the air. I guessed they were having a fistfight but I could not see past the shadow of men that still stood around me.

Two other men stepped up to take their place and started a commentary of their own. They were hard to understand and spoke in a mishmash of modern day language, along with the unmistakable brogue of a Scotsman and something else I couldn't figure out. I could only get bits and pieces of the conversation.

"Och, she stinks." Alec pinched his nose.

"Aye, that she does," Graham agreed taking a step back. His dark blonde hair stood on end. He grabbed hold of the length and tethered it with a piece of leather.

"We should toss her in the Loch and see if she comes clean," Alec suggested. He was only three and twenty but he was already six feet tall.

"How ye going to get her there?" asked Muir, coming back from his fistfight with Callum, straightening his kilt.

"Ye can carry her," Graham said, as he adjusted the hilt of his sword. "I won't be the one lifting her up smelling the way she does."

Muir looked indignant at such an idea. "Why can't ye two do it?"

"We are older," Alec said, as though this explained everything.

"Who's doing what?" asked Callum, stepping into the circle once more.

"Ye will take the lass to the Loch with Muir's help and see if she comes clean."

"Can I take off her clothes?"

Alec looked at Graham, who looked at Muir, who looked down at the girl in the mud. "How'd ye know she is even wearing clothes?"

Callum shrugged.

I tried to say something, but no words would come out.

"Look, she *is* alive?" Muir pointed his finger. "Her mouth is moving?"

"Cease all of ye," Gavin said, his voice deep with a heavy brogue combined with a hint of an English accent. "Pick her up and dump her in the

Loch. If she comes clean and is toothsome, we will keep her. If not, leave her there."

"It is cold," Callum argued. "She may catch her death."

"What do I care? I have no use for another ugly crone slowing us down. Now get on with it." Gavin stepped forward and leaned down to look at the person in the mud.

Blinking, I stared up into the loveliest pair of eyes for a man that I had ever seen. They were a cross between green and blue. And even though the color was strange, yet beautiful, I had the distinct feeling I had seen that very same color somewhere before, but for the life of me, I couldn't remember where. They mesmerized me until he frowned and wrinkled his nose in displeasure before covering his face. Some part of me finally came back to my senses. Out of sheer determination, I tried to sit up but only managed to move a little before I was sucked back into my prison of filth.

"Ye take her arms; I'll grab her feet." Callum walked over to the edge of the pit.

Hands grabbed at my body none too carefully and yanked me from the vat of filth that had me trapped.

Moving quickly, the two men held my arms and legs while running up a rocky incline, picking up speed as they descended the other side. I felt like I was going to be ripped in two.

"On the count of three…" one of them yelled over the howling wind.

"Three."

My body swung outward and released.

I was airborne for a split second and then submerged completely into frigid water.

The skirts I wore weighed me down. I kicked my feet, struggling to rise back to the surface. With a final kick, I broke out from the barrier of water. A heavy fog was on the top. Gasping for air, I swam back toward the shore out of sheer determination.

Dripping wet and shivering, I found purchase on the rocks below and climbed from the water.

The two men/boys that had thrown me into the water stood there with widened eyes.

"*Bastards!*" I sputtered, swiping my wet hair from my face.

"What did she say?" Callum asked.

"I believe she called ye a bastard," Muir responded.

"How do ye know she was speaking ta me and not ye?"

"Ye are a bastard," Muir reminded him and crossed his arms. "I am not."

"Ye will be when I get through with ye," Callum warned, balling his fists.

"Not likely."

"What is the matter with you?" I chattered, so mad, I was seeing red.

"Aye she is a feisty one, full of spit and vinegar," Muir stated.

"We did just throw her in the Loch. It would seem she may have good reason for calling us such," Callum noted.

"Aye, I can see why she may be mad. Think ye she is toothsome enough for the Laird?" asked the one with the long hair. He had the pretty face of a boy not fully matured.

"Aye," said the taller of the two, his face was older but just as handsome. His eyes slowly raked over the gown that clung to my body like saran wrap.

"The lass looks mighty fine ta me." Callum let out a low appreciative whistle.

"Good birthing hips on that one." Muir nodded his agreement.

Both men examined me as I stood shivering by the shore, having a heated conversation that I understood very little. A large white bird flew overhead, squawking loudly, then dove into the water and came back out with a fish writhing in its long beak. Their attention momentarily diverted on the bird, I grabbed up my sopping wet skirts and tried to run. Unfortunately, I was so cold I could barely get my legs to work.

"Where do ye think she is going?" asked Callum, watching her departing form as she tried to run over the rock-laden embankment.

"I don't know but ye better get her before she falls and hurts herself on the rocks," Muir suggested.

"Would our laird want her looking the way that she does?" Callum asked, reassessing her as she ran forward. Her calves were shapely but a little smaller than he would have imagined due to the size of her bosom.

"Aye, I believe he would." Muir watched the aforementioned bosom bouncing up and down as she ran. "Well, what are ye waiting for? Go and get her."

"I am not doing it myself," Callum argued. "She is mad."

Stopping, I gave up trying to run away, turned back around, and stomped back to the men who were more boys. I had no idea where I was, so running away was not going to help me in the least. "You heathens give me something to wear." I was shivering uncontrollably.

The sound of my voice brought their eyes back to me as they stood there looking confused.

"What is she saying?" Callum asked out of the side of his mouth.

"I don't know," Muir said.

Rubbing my arms, I stood there shivering waiting for them to do something. When neither came to my aide, I walked up to the smallest one. "I am borrowing this." I tugged the plaid.

"I think she wants yer extra plaid, Callum," Muir said.

"Aye, I think she does." Callum released his extra plaid to the girl and then stood back.

Wrapping the plaid around my body, I tried to get warm but it did little since my clothing was so wet.

"Take yer clothes off, lass," Muir said.

Somehow, I understood that. "I will do no such thing."

"That is the only way ye will get warm, lass." He shrugged his broad shoulders.

With the numbness settling in my limbs, my legs gave out. My head hit the rocks before my body and I promptly blacked out.

CHAPTER TWO

Alec tucked his reddish-brown hair behind his ears as he bent over to look behind a scraggly bush. A long twisting ringlet fell forward over his broad shoulder, which looked out of place on a man his size. "Do ye see a basket?"

"No," Graham said, looking just as hard. He wandered over to a large boulder, and glanced behind it.

"Mayhap she misplaced it," Alec offered.

"Och, where though?" asked Graham.

"How do I know," Alec said as he straightened once more. "I wonder if she is going to be comely."

Graham made a snorting noise. "She better hope so. Laird Grey said if Morag sends us another one of those ugly ones, we will tether her near the loch and use her as an offering for the monster."

Alec shook his head morosely. "Aye, let's hope she is toothsome."

Callum and Muir struggled up the hill with their burden in tow.

Gavin stepped forward and pushed his hair back as it pitched forward in the bristling wind. "What happened to her?"

"She fell on the rocks and hit her head," Callum and Muir both blurted at the same time.

"How did she manage that?" Gavin gave his men a cold stare.

Both young men shrugged and shook their heads, looking at each other. "Tis slippery by the loch," they explained.

Gavin rolled his eyes. "Tis growing late," he said. "Toss her on a horse and let's make our way back ta the keep before the storm is upon us."

"It was sunny a few moments ago," Callum noted. "Think ye this is an omen of what is ta come?"

Gavin tensed. He was tired of all this superstitious talk. Even though he was partially to blame for it—he had to keep his men in line one way or another. "Only if ye do not get her on that horse and get moving."

"What does that have ta do with an omen?" Muir asked looking bewildered.

"Ye will get wet and so will she." Gavin swung on his horse.

"Do ye want to carry her with ye?" Callum lifted her limp arm in the air.

Gavin looked at the dripping wet girl and pulled his own plaid closer to his shoulders against the frigid wind. "No."

"Think ye she is comely enough?" Muir asked, hopefully.

"Aye, she looks better now." He nodded his head. "I had my doubts it was even a girl." Thunder boomed in the distance. "She will do....*for now*," he added as an afterthought and reined his horse around, heading back for home.

They didn't beat the storm. Every man was drenched by the time they made it back. One by one, the thirteen men filed inside the keep, dripping a goodly amount of water on the filthy rushes.

That was surely one way to get the rushes clean, Gavin mused. He looked over his shoulder at the girl hanging between Callum and Muir. "Take her ta my chamber."

"Do ye want her on yer bed?" asked Callum shifting her legs under his arms.

"God no!" Gavin shook his head. "Put her on the floor." He stood there waiting but neither of the boys had moved. "What?" He glared at them.

"Do we put something on the floor? It tis awfully chilly in here," Callum said, shifting uncomfortably.

"Ye can use one of the older furs." Gavin exhaled. "Not the good ones...understand?"

"Yes." Callum and Muir both nodded.

Gavin widened his eyes. "What are ye waiting for? Take her upstairs."

Both Muir and Callum carried her up the stairs.

Gavin only saw them hit her head twice on the way up - that was something, he supposed.

"Look at what ye have done, Callum." Muir shook his head disparagingly. "Now he is in a bad way."

"Me?" Callum gasped. "I just asked whether we should put the lass on the cold floor. Think ye he would have a care with this new one since he nearly killed the last one before he sent her off." He shook his head morosely. "She made good bread, though." Callum swallowed hard. "Where'd ye think he sent her ta?"

Muir shook his head. "I don't know and I don't think I want ta truly find out."

Callum gasped. "Think ye he sent her ta the loch?"

"That is just a silly superstition," Muir said trying to keep the quivering edge from his voice.

"If it's just a silly superstition, why is yer voice shaking like a wee scared lassie?"

"Ye'll be sorry for that." Muir dropped his burden and made a lunge for Callum.

Callum did the same and jumped across the room, dodging Muir. Back and forth, they faced off against one another, ducking, lunging, and exchanging blows with each other.

"Cease both of ye," Alec yelled as he came to stand inside the door. "By the saints above, ye stupid fools, I think ye have broken her."

Both Callum and Muir looked down at the girl.

Callum bent over, straightened the strange crick in her leg, and tossed an old fur on top of her. He shoved his hand through his hair. "What? She looks fine ta me."

Muir crossed his arms. "Callum, think ye we should put the fur underneath her?"

"Ye both better hope she wakes up, if not Laird Grey will have both yer heads on a platter and be serving them up as an offering to the monster of Loch Morar.

"Och, Muir, ye lied." Callum shivered. "The monster does exist."

Muir shrugged. "How do I know? I have never seen a monster in the Loch."

Callum's eyes widened. "We have a monster in *our* Loch?"

Alec rolled his eyes. "Where do ye think all the people go?"

"Ta another town."

"Ye keep telling yerself that Callum." Alec shook his head and walked out of the room.

Callum looked at Muir. "We should probably put the fur under her like ye said."

"Can we use more than one fur?" Muir asked.

"I don't think we should, Laird Grey said ta use the bad one. He didn't say anything about two bad ones."

Muir looked over at the bed skeptically. "They all look in a bad way ta me, how'd ye know which one ta take?"

"It was easy," Callum boasted. "I took the one with the least amount of fur on it."

Muir sighed and shook his head. "Come on, let's roll her over on the fur before Laird Grey comes and sees the mess we made."

"Och, is she bleeding then?" Callum asked, leaning over, pushing her hair away from her face.

Muir bent down and did a quick inspection of her head. "Not anymore." He stood up. "I'm sure it was just a scratch anyway. Remember she hit her own head by the Loch."

Callum's eyes widened. "Think ye Alec is telling the truth about the monster?"

Muir shook his head. "I don't know and I am not in any hurry ta find out."

"Why do ye think we haven't heard about this fierce monster before now?"

Muir shrugged. "Mayhap it wasn't time ta feed it."

CHAPTER THREE

The expanse of a very chiseled naked torso was the first thing I saw when the darkness receded. Blinking, I tried to focus my eyes better as it was a very fine looking chest, and if I was dreaming, I wanted to memorize every inch.

A large tub was placed in the center of a rather spacious stone room… well… it was more like a barrel, with cloths draped over the sides.

Steam emitted from the top.

The rest of his clothing fell to the floor.

He turned towards me.

My eyes popped. *Wow.*

A flush of heat burned my face. I swallowed hard. Who the heck was he? I felt like I should pinch myself to make sure I was awake, but then again, if I was dreaming, I wasn't altogether sure I wanted to wake up...

"Are ye planning on feasting yer eyes on my fine form all day?" He lifted a dark brow.

His heavy brogue rolled off his tongue and I couldn't understand a word. I lifted my eyes to his face and my breath caught. I remembered him immediately. His blue-green gaze, unforgettable, never wavered. "Uh, what did you say?"

He exhaled heavily and scrubbed his hands over his face. "I said," he articulated with a surprisingly less amount of brogue. "Come, wash my back woman. I do not have all day." He climbed into the tub and sat down.

Once his body was submerged and out of my line of view, my sense came back. "Excuse me?"

My temper flared. How rude! "I'll have you know…whoever you are. I am not your personal back scrubber." Turning in a huff, I crossed the room, grabbed hold of the handle on the large wooden door in front of me and yanked. "Heathen," I muttered under my breath.

"Where are ye headed lass?" he sighed audibly, lifting his leg and splashing water over the top.

I turned back around. "I'm going to get my money back, that's where I'm headed," I informed him using my sternest voice and turned back towards the door.

"Yer money?" He made a snorting noise. "I don't think ye will have much luck finding yer coin at this juncture, lass."

"Wanna bet?" I whirled back to face him and once again, I was taken aback by how handsome he was. At least the gypsy got that part right.

"Leave if ye like, but if ye stay ye *will* wash my back." He lifted his brow as though he was daring me to say otherwise.

"I think I'll take my chances," I informed him.

"Suit yerself."

Not having any other option at this point, I headed out of his room into the drafty stone hallway. Wrapping my arms around my stomach, I followed the sound of voices to the top of the stairs. The room below was filled with men, all of who were in various stages of undress. I counted them and there were twelve total that I could see. Two smaller versions of the tub I had just seen were in front of the large fireplace. The men were pulling sticks and then laughing. I remembered the one boy from earlier. He and his friend were the ones that threw me into that damn water. He pulled out a short stick and by the look on his face, he wasn't very happy with his draw.

Not having any other choice, I took a reviving breath and headed down the stairs. However, the closer I came to the bottom I felt I might have been a bit hasty in my decision to vacate the premises. Not one of the men said a word to me or bothered to cover up.

It was hard not to stare but somehow I managed to keep my eyes on the door across the hall, although I could certainly see plenty in my peripheral

A heady musky smell resonated in the room accompanied by a light scent of Lavender. Neither belonged in such close proximity to the other and yet, somehow, I found it to be a pleasing aroma just the same. Once across the room, I grabbed hold of the cold metal handle, pushed through the doors and stepped outside. *"Oh Hell!*

"Where'd ye think she is going?" asked Callum.

"The same place they all go," Muir said, wiping down the blade of his dirk with a cloth.

"Where might that be?" whispered Callum, leaning forward.

"Ta take a gander outside, I suppose."

"Why would she do that?" asked Callum, his brow creased in confusion. "Tis too dark ta see anything at this hour—the moon is not even shining."

"Och, tis nothing new, the lass will be back shortly," said Muir.

"How'd ye know, Muir? Can ye read minds now, is that it?" Callum crossed his arms indignantly.

"Mayhap I can," Muir laughed and cuffed him on his ear. "Tis dark Callum and the last time I checked no wee lass is going ta want to stay out in the night pitched in blackness alone, at least not for verra long."

"Well, I don't think she's coming back."

"Ye care ta place a small wager then," asked Muir.

"What do ye want ta bet?"

"I will bet yer second helpings at breakfast."

"My second helpings?" Callum made a face. "Och that is too steep a price ta pay for such a thing. What do I get if I am right and ye are wrong?"

"Ye can have my second helpings at breakfast for an entire week."

"A week ye say?" Callum crossed his arms and stroked his chin, thinking. "I want yer turn bathing as well," Callum added as an afterthought.

Muir shrugged. "Suit yerself but if we are betting that as well, I also get your turn bathing if the stick ye pulled is better than the one I pull."

"Fine, it is a deal then," Callum said.

"Alec, will ye bear witness ta this bet?" Muir asked.

"Aye, why not," he said, stepping up to take his turn in the tub. The water was already a light shade of brown. He unbelted his kilt, draped it over the back of a chair, and climbed inside. Reaching up he pulled a strip of leather from his hair; the length fell in soft waves down his back as he settled down into the water.

"Well?" Muir held out his hand.

Callum reached out and took his hand. "Yes, we have a deal." They shook hands then turned toward the door and waited.

CHAPTER FOUR

"Way to go, Paige!" I threw my hands up in the air and couldn't even see them. It didn't go unnoticed to me that the room I had just walked through looked like it should be in another era, as did the several men in various stages of undress. And now, with nothing but blackness in front of me, the idea of scrubbing off the back of a Highlander... err...

correction... a *very* handsome Highlander, who also had a *very* broad, muscular back...

A strange scraping sound cut through the darkness like a knife. I turned, but I couldn't see where it was coming from, let alone see what it was.

"Oh hell!"

Not having any better options at the moment, I reached out in the darkness until my hand closed over the cool metal handle. Jerking open the door, I headed back inside the castle. Once again, my view was of several men in various stages of undress. My eyes flitted to the left and then the right as I hustled quickly across the room. When I reached the stairs, I lifted my skirts and practically ran the rest of the way to *his* door.

"Ha!" Muir slapped Callum on the back. "I told ye she would be back."

Callum brooded.

"What's this, Callum?" Muir peered closely at his face.

"Och, Muir, if I didn't know better I'd think ye cheated."

Muir made a disgusted grunt. "I didn't know ye were such a sore loser Callum." He shook his head. "It doesn't matter anyway," he said. "I still get yer second helpings at breakfast for the next week."

Callum's eyes boggled. "I didn't say ye could have my second helpings for an entire week."

"Ye did too," Muir argued.

"No." Callum adamantly shook his head back and forth. "I said ye could have one of my second helpings at breakfast and ye said if I won I would get a week of yer second helpings at breakfast."

"Och, Callum..." Muir shook his head solemnly. "I never figured ye for a liar."

"Take that back Muir," Callum snapped, putting his fists up. "I will not have ye sully my good name," he spat. "And if ye don't take back what ye said I will be forced to seek retribution."

Muir crossed his arms. "And what retribution might that be, Callum?"

"I WI—will'," Callum sputtered. "Put my boot right up yer hairy arse."

Muir scoffed. "Try it Callum and I will cuff yer ears again and make ye cry like a wee girl like I did the last time ye tried ta fight with me."

Alec rose from the tub. "Cease both of ye else I will be the one shoving my boot up both ye arse's."

Callum gave Muir a smug look of satisfaction.

Alec stepped over the rim of the tub and used a drying cloth to remove the excess water and few pieces of debris that had settled on his muscular thighs from the bath. He looked at Callum. "I witnessed the bet. Ye have to give Muir yer second helpings at breakfast and now, yer turn bathing as well." He lifted his plaid, tossed it over his shoulder, and walked away from the tub.

Callum looked over at the water. It was an even darker shade of brown than before. He shook his head. He'd be lucky if he even got clean now.

The door to *his* room was slightly ajar. I peeked through the opening, watching. His head was back against the rim of the makeshift tub and his hair fell over the side.

The gypsy's words came back to me…

"Take the basket of offerings lass, ta the top of the mountain, cross over the screaming bridge ta the other side and the Highlander ye seek will come fer ye."

At the time, I was still a bit drunk, wallowing in an ample amount of self-pity and being a mite fanciful. I wanted a Highlander and if I had to carry a basket across a screaming bridge, a mile up in the air to the top of the mountain and wait for him to come for me, I didn't see anything wrong with it…well not terribly wrong. However, the old bat never said anything about being a ….once again her words came back to haunt me.

"Be careful what ye wish for lass, it jes might come true."

I looked across the room with new eyes. It was an adequate room, that is, if you were living in a castle in the past. The sparse furnishing scattered throughout consisted of a large four-posted bed, filled with numerous furs, with a rather sizeable trunk at the bottom that looked like it should be filled with treasure, a table with a chair and a rather pretty screen with paintings of animals and fauna over in the far corner. I couldn't see what was behind it.

"Lass come inside and shut the door."

The sound of his voice startled me.

"How did you know I was here?" I walked through the door and shut it, just as he instructed.

"I could hear yer breathing from across the room. I kept waiting for ye ta hit the floor."

"Why would I hit the floor?"

He turned and lifted his brow a notch. "From swooning," he explained.

"Swooning?" I gaped. "Why would I do such a thing?"

"Ye were ogling my body with yer eyes, I could sense it."

"Oh, please," I scoffed. "Get over yourself." Even though that was exactly what I was doing.

He gave me a doubtful look. "There is no need to tell lie's ta me, lass."

"I am not...." Oh, what was the point? I gave up. He was right. I was lying. "Where am I... exactly?"

"Ye are in Greystone Castle, lass."

"I know I am in a damn castle!" I stomped my foot in irritation.

He gave me a warning glance. "There is no need to vent yer anger at me, lass. Obviously ye are the one who signed the contract."

That took the wind out of my sails. I did sign the contract but what bothered me was how he even knew about it.

"I can see ye are surprised I know about the contract, aye?"

I merely nodded my head.

"Ye must have signed or ye would no be here. Now ye are bound ta me."

"Bound?"

"Aye, lass." He exhaled as though he was tiring of our conversation. "Did ye sign the contract with ye own blood?"

"Well...yes."

"Then what is the problem?"

"Well..." I wasn't sure how to answer that. What was my problem? I did ask for a Highlander and here one was right in front of me, looking better than I could have ever imagined...

Now that he put it that way, I wasn't sure why I was so upset. Well, besides the obvious reasons. I thought, well, I wasn't real sure what I thought, other than being a bit too drunk to think clearly at the time.

"I thought it wasn't real," I finally said.

He laughed. It was a hearty sound and warmed me immediately. "If ye thought it wasn't real, then why on God's green Earth did ye sign the contract, lass?"

Stupidity.

Scratch that.

That wasn't the truth. The truth was… it was wishful thinking that made me sign the contract. I wanted a Highlander and wished for one, and like the gypsy said, I now have one right here in front of me. Now that I compartmentalized it, I really had no idea what my problem was. I should be ecstatic, not partially irritated and the other part…freaking out. (Well, maybe I should be freaking out a bit) I amended.

"Where are we…well, other than in a castle?"

He cupped his hands, slid them into the water, and splashed it over his face. Wiping the excess away with one hand, he turned to look at me. Droplets of water lingered on his long lashes and the faint scruff of stubble on his face. "We are in Scotland, lass."

I swallowed hard. "Scotland, you say?" I pressed my hand to my mouth. "That can't be right," I said more to myself than him.

"Ye look peaked, lass," he noted as he looked at me once again over his very nicely sculpted shoulder.

"Who *are* you?" Even though I tried to keep the quivering edge from my voice, it still came out more of a squeak.

"Gavin de Grey," he said. "I am the current laird o' Greystone Castle." He cocked his head to the side. "Ye may call me, Laird."

"Oh—kay, Laird," I choked out as my heart jumped into double time. "What century is this?"

His dark brows creased as he gave me a confused look.

"What year?" I nearly shouted.

His expression remained surprisingly impassive.

I switched tactics. "Who is your King?"

"That depends on who ye ask." His brow lifted another notch.

"Who is the current King?"

He made a face and exhaled as he sunk against the back of the tub. "King James."

"Oh." I kneeled on the floor, gripping the side of tub to keep me upright. I wasn't great with history but I did know if James was King, I was in the past. Apparently, the damn gypsy hadn't been lying after all.

"If ye want to find a real Highlander do ye mind traveling to a different time lass?"

I remembered very clearly, hiccupping as I leaned closer on the table. *"Meh-sure, why not,"* I told her, playing along.

"Are ye sure, lass?" Her rheumy eyes sparkled mischievously like she had a big secret.

"Yep," I had said and I recalled a wink to boot.

"Oh hell," I groaned, leaning forward.

"Do ye need to relieve yerself, lass?"

I looked up. The instant our eyes met, I felt like I may need to lie down, for like ever. Apparently, he was not immune either for in that moment he looked like he might need to lie down as well.

"No."

"Well if ye are going ta be sick ye might want ta use the chamber pot in the corner," he suggested helpfully as he leaned away from me in the tub. I would have laughed at his horrified expression but...I heaved and ran to the aforementioned pot.

Gripping the sides of the bowl, I leaned over and was surprised nothing came out. When I was sure I wasn't going to be sick, I ducked out from behind the screen and walked back across the room.

"Have ye finally figured out ye are somewhere ye wouldn't have thought ta be?" Both his brows lifted this time as though he was accentuating his point.

I nodded my head, accepting my fate. I tried not to think of the impossibility of the situation or that I just might be out of my ever-loving-freaking mind.

He seemed to ponder this for a moment and then sank back against the tub, once again. Steam rose in the air and a light sheen of perspiration was on his face. There was no doubt about one thing, he was a mighty fine Highlander and I did ask for one—maybe this wouldn't be so bad after all....right? I could stay here for a while... a mini vacation of sorts, and then go back home.

He cracked open one eye and lifted a perfectly arched brow. "What are ye waiting for, lass?"

"What?" I looked back at his handsome face. He was giving me another one of his curious looks.

"I said," he said slowing his words so I could understand. "Wash the filth from my body before the water gets cold."

I understood him that time. "All rightly then," I muttered. Blowing my hair from my eyes, I reached over the side of the tub to grab the soap floating on top. My fingers barely closed over the rectangle bar before a firm hand grabbed hold of my own.

"Take care with that soap. Tis the only one I have left," he said. I got the gist of what he was saying that time and he didn't even slow his mishmash of words. Once again, I was reminded of words from modern day sprinkled, off and on, with Scottish words and old English.

I tugged on my hand. He gave me the hairy eyeball, a warning of sorts I supposed, and released me. I frowned at the soap. It was purple.

Purple? "Where did you get this?" I felt like I had just entered into an episode of the Twilight Zone.

He reclined back in the water, shutting his eyes once more. "One of the previous witches left it for me." Lifting his hand, he slid it back through his wet hair.

"Why'd she do that?" A sudden flare of jealously shot through me—he was supposed to be *my* highlander.

He lifted his massive shoulders and lowered them. "It was an offering, so I might spare her life and send her back home," he explained.

"What?" I gaped. "Wait...an offering?"

"Yer a witch too, are ye not?" He slanted an eye open.

"That depends on what you do with witches," I hedged. Standing up from the floor, I glanced around the room looking for an escape route if the need arose.

"In another time we would burn them but I have seen far too many things of late and actually the stench of burning flesh really bothers me."

"Ah, what did you do with this other witch?"

"I suppose she went back ta where she came from, but she left this for me." He held up the soap. "What did ye bring me? More soap? Candies? Or did ye bring me some other wonder from the future to fill my belly?"

"What?"

"Ye are from another time are ye not?

"Well...," I chewed on my lip, pulling it between my teeth. "*Maaybe*?"

"This conversation is tedious." He closed his eyes. "I am waiting."

"For what...exactly?"

"For ye ta wash me." He exhaled and cracked open his eye again.

Not having any options at this point, I stepped forward. "Uh, okay."

I walked around to the bottom of the tub, reached into the water, and lifted his foot. It was a very large foot. He pulled it back down and water splashed up over the front of my gown that had just recently dried out from my earlier drenching.

"Are ye daft?"

"What is with you people calling me daft?" I recognized the word from earlier, not to mention the numerous historical romances I had read.

"Ye will want ta start with my hair and then work yer way down my body."

"How silly of me," I muttered and made my way back up to the top of the tub.

"There is a pitcher over there." He inclined his head to the opposite side of the room. "Ye may use it to rinse my hair, and there is some shampoo as well, lavender I think."

"Lavender?" I gaped at him in shock.

"Aye…" He gave me a pointed look. "Is there a problem?"

"No…" I shook my head. "Not at all," I said. Now I knew why the hall below had smelled like lavender.

"I like the way it smells," he explained and closed his eyes once more.

"Of course you do." I didn't know why this didn't surprise me more.

"Come now, lass, and get ta it before the water gets cold." He lifted his foot up and propped it on the edge of the tub.

Standing, I wiped my hands on my already wet gown and got the pitcher from the table. When I turned around he was giving me a strange look and my belly flip-flopped. Ignoring him and the giddy rush of excitement flowing through me, I returned to the side of the tub and set the pitcher on the floor. "So…" I hedged as I lifted up the bottle of shampoo and poured out handful of liquid.

He slanted an eye open. "Yes…"

"How often do you bathe?"

"Depends…" he said and shut his eye.

"On…"

"Whether I need ta bathe or not." He muttered something else that was hard to hear but I could swear he used the word daft again.

Irritated, I smacked the glob of shampoo down of his head and vigorously rubbed it into his long hair.

"How long were ye waiting for me?" His voice was pleasant and deep—very sexy.

"What?"

"Ye were waiting for me were ye not?"

"Uh..." I flustered and knocked the shampoo on the floor.

"Och, lass, careful. That is the only bottle I have."

Grabbing hold of the wayward bottle, I set it upright on the floor and resumed rubbing the shampoo through his hair. The silky mass slid through my fingers.

"How long were ye waiting for me?" he asked again.

"I'm not sure what you're asking me?" Distracted, my eyes floated back down to the water lapping just below his navel.

"Looking for something?" He lifted the soap from the water where my eyes were stuck.

"Thanks." I took it from his hand. "No, I don't think so." I reached up and felt my head. Did I have a concussion?

"Are ye always this slow then?"

"What?" I gaped at him. "I'm not slow." My voice came out all screechy. "Why would you say such a thing?"

"It seems that way ta me." He shrugged his broad shoulders.

"*Jerk.*"

"Ah, another one of your strange words from the future I suppose." He sighed. "Ye want to go back into the bog of mud?"

"No."

"Well..." He lifted his brow. "Then make yerself useful."

"Fine," I gritted. Grabbing the pitcher, I dunked it into the water a bit forcefully.

He pushed back against the tub. "Och, lass, are ye trying to make me a eunuch?"

I finally noticed where I submerged the pitcher. It was right below his navel. "Oops, sorry," I said sheepishly and quickly pulled out the pitcher that was now filled with water and set it down beside the tub.

He slid back down into the water but not before I got another really good eyeful of his incredible physique.

"So does this happen often?" I resumed rubbing his scalp. It was kind-of a turn on.

"Does what happen often?" He sounded like he was from modern day again.

I shook my head, not sure what to make of his mish-mashed language. He turned and looked up at me. "You know," I said. "Getting girls from the future?" I elaborated, suddenly hoping that wasn't the case.

"Not often," he said and this time I noticed his brow twitched. Was that a tell? Was he lying?

"How did you know where to get me?"

"I ventured through the mist and retrieved ye," he explained. "Ye were exactly where the crone, I mean the uh, gypsy, told me you would be."

"How would she know?"

He shrugged. "Can't say. She wanted ta make a trade though and ye were it—this time," he muttered under his breath.

"What was that?" I stopped rubbing his scalp.

He exhaled heavily. "She said if we let her go through the mist another lass would be there waiting for us." He smiled up at me. "She said ye would be much younger and toothsome."

There was a glint in his eye and I swallowed hard. "Toothsome?"

Of course, I read enough romance novels to know what toothsome meant but I wanted him to tell me.

"Aye, it merely means ye are easy ta look at."

"Well, am I?" I prodded, suddenly feeling unaccountably warmer than I had moments before.

He stared at me for a moment and then nodded. "I suppose ye will do...*for now*."

My entire body went rigid and I had a sudden urge to dunk him under the water.

"Get ta work, lass. I am tired and the water is growing cold."

Really? The water was scolding my damn hands. I scratched his scalp harder.

"That feels nice."

Figures.

CHAPTER FIVE

"This is how it works," he said, pacing back and forth in front of me, his long strides making quick work of the distance between each wall in the room. He pivoted with his hands clasped behind his back and walked to the other side of the room. "Ye will stay with me… for a time…"

"Excuse me." I lifted my hand in the air. We had been at this for quite a while now.

He paused and turned. "Aye," he sighed.

"How long will I be here?" I adjusted my position on the trunk; the little rivets were poking me in my left butt cheek.

"I do not know."

"How long was the last one here?"

"I cannot recall." His eyes shifted to the side — a sure sign he was lying.

"Was it a long time, like years?" I watched his reaction closely.

"Not that I recall," he deflected again and sure enough, his eyes shot over to the side. He cleared his throat. "As I was saying…" He resumed his pacing. "Yer stay can be pleasurable or it can be, well…"

"Well, what?"

"Ye will see."

I wasn't real sure what to make of this. I lifted my hand in the air again, waving it around to get his attention. "What's your name, again?"

He stopped once more. "Gavin de Grey, the current laird of this fine piece o' rock."

"So this is Greystone castle, right?" I didn't know why that name rang a bell with me. I felt like I heard about it before.

"Aye, it is." He shifted, turning towards the window.

"Why does your name sound English?"

"I *am* part English." He gave me an exasperated look.

Well, excuse me, I felt like saying. How in the heck was I supposed to know that? "Oh. Wait...how can you be laird if you aren't a full-fledged Scotsman?"

"Lass," he sighed. "A Laird is nothing more than a person ta look ta in a time of need. The ruler or owner of a piece o' land, and with luck, a home as well.

"Oh." I wished I had studied history more. The only reason why I knew about any of this was from reading romances—not the best resource for fact.

"I can tell there is something else ye wish ta ask me." His dark brows rose.

"Well, I was wondering why you sound so...."

He stepped closer and my heart did another involuntary flutter.

"So..."

"What is yer name?" he asked derailing my train of thought.

"Paige Walsh."

"Paige Walsh," he repeated. "It has a nice ring ta it, I suppose."

"Thanks," I deadpanned.

"Where do ye hail from, Paige Walsh?"

"Huh?

"Where do ye come from, Paige Walsh?"

"You can call me Paige."

"Paige, then," he said as though trying it on for size as he awaited my response.

"America."

He nodded his head, seemingly accepting my answer.

"What is your name again?" I already knew of course, but I liked the way he said it.

"Gavin de Grey, the Laird o' this fine piece o' rock."

"May I call you Gavin?

"Nay, lass." He shook his head.

"How about Grey?" Grey was a pretty-sexy name.

He shook his head again. "Nay, lass."

"What should I call you then?"

"I thought it was obvious." His eyes slid into a roll and suddenly I wanted to kick him.

"If it was obvious, I wouldn't have asked." My voice came out harsher than I intended but his arrogant demeanor was getting on my nerves.

"Ye may call me, Laird."

"Unbelievable." I threw up my hands.

He gave me a stern look and then resumed his pacing. It seemed the formalities were at an end because he resumed giving me instructions once again.

"Now..." He gave me a pointed look as he paced. "Ye will cook, clean, and wash my body..." He ticked each task off on his fingers one by one. "And if ye are fortunate and I deem it so..." He stopped in front of me and leaned down so close I could see the rings of sapphire surrounding the emerald colored iris of his eyes. "I will also let ye tend me…in bed…" His warm breath wafted over me as the tips of his fingers gently stroked my cheek. Shivers of delight raced over my skin, not only from the action but from the way he spoke, smooth and velvety, like a decadent piece of candy, and it took just about everything I had in me not to lean in closer as his sexy smoldering gaze lifted from my face to the aforementioned bed behind me.

His words finally registered, I shook some sense back into my mushy brain.

"Wow."

I couldn't believe his arrogance. Who did he think I was? As if I would just tumble into bed with him. Not likely. But even as I thought it, I couldn't help wondering what it would be like. And by the looks of him, it would be pretty damn fantastic.

"I know, lass," he said, as if reading my thoughts. "I am a generous partner in bed and have yet ta hear any complaints." He added a sly smile that nearly knocked the breath I didn't realize I was holding from my lungs.

That faded though, and in its place a rush of anger shot through me at his audacity. "Of all the egotistical, arrogant, conceited…"

His smile faded quickly, replaced by a scowl. He dropped his hand and stepped away from me. "Ye can always sleep on the floor." He flung out his arm indicating the rumpled fur in front of the fire. "Makes no never mind ta me."

"Wait…what?" My stomach flipped over on itself at the look of pain that entered his eyes for a brief moment.

"If ye find me so displeasing…" his velvety voice took on a harsh edge as his eyes hardened against mine. "Ye can sleep on the floor," he repeated and shrugged his broad shoulders like he could care less.

That was such a quick turnaround, I felt like I had whiplash. I guessed my face showed my shock because his lips turned up at the corners, just a hint. Was he smirking at me?

"I will even give ye one o' the furs from my bed, not the good ones, o' course."

"O' course," I mimicked with a hefty amount of sarcasm and a large dollop of disbelief at how quickly the conversation had veered from tending him in bed to sleeping on the floor, alone.

"Ye may also bathe in the water once I have finished," he told me and pointed to the now empty tub. "I am finished now, so ye should bathe as well." He crossed his arms. "See, I am not… inhospitable." He gave me a small but meaningful smile.

My blistering rebuttal puttered out at the sight of *that* smile. I was done for. "*Great.*"

CHAPTER SIX

s I stood over the tub, watching the steam rise, I decided a quick bath wouldn't be such a bad thing. Peeling off my wet clothing, I dropped them to the floor. Besides, he didn't leave me much choice. It was either bathe up here, or down in the hall with his men. Luckily for me, he had matters to attend to, so I was alone to bathe in peace. Bracing my hands on either side of the tub, I slid down into the water. The burning heat immediately warmed my chilled body. I was amazed it was still so hot. Leaning back against the rim of the tub, the water soothed my aching, everything

Unfortunately, it did little to soothe my brain, which was spinning a mile a minute. How did I get here? How many women had that damn gypsy sent here? How was any of this even possible? Maybe I hit my head harder than I thought and was now having some kind of concussion induced hallucination… except, I didn't hit my head until I was already here.

"Oh hell!"

Not able to come up with any real answers to the deluge of questions swirling through my mind, I vigorously scrubbed my body with the pathetic sliver of hard soap he deemed worthy for me to use. I noticed he also took the shampoo along with the large bar of soap I had used on him and locked it in the trunk at the bottom of the bed. Lifting up the tiny sliver of soap, I tried my best to wash my hair.

Gavin sat in his usual chair at the head of the table in the great hall as he and his men made quick work of finishing off one of the last remaining barrels of ale they had stolen from one of the neighboring towns.

Well, it wasn't stealing per se, he amended, but a lengthy borrow until such time they could replace it with another. Of course, they had nothing to replace it with, so, it would be a really, really, lengthy borrow. But once they had the treasure, he would pay them back tenfold, or so he often told his nagging conscience, time and again to assuage his guilt. The problem, as it had been from the beginning, was getting the treasure out of the cave away from the serpent or 'the monster', of the Loch. Now that was the quandary. How did one go about getting a treasure from a monster that he had never seen and sincerely doubted even existed?

The crone had told him it was real, as real as the mist she had disappeared through. The same mist he had gotten the lass from, in exchange for the latest witches' freedom. She also told him if he stuck to his end of the bargain, he would be able to retrieve the treasure. But how did one go about sacrificing someone to a monster?

At the time, he would have agreed to anything...but now, he had to wonder if the treasure was even worth it? His empty belly said yes, but his mind and heart had different ideas. He squelched down that foreboding thought, burying it deep into his subconscious to attend to at such time he would need to retrieve it.

Besides, he sincerely doubted it would even come to that because he couldn't seem to find the bloody monster in the first place. So now, what was he to do with the lass?

Keep her?

She was comely enough, he supposed, that is, he amended, when she kept her shrewish mouth shut. Aye, she did have a quick temper, he thought, as he remembered how her amber eyes had ignited with fury when he told her to wash the filth from his body.

He chuckled aloud with the remembrance, which garnered a few curious looks from his men. He ignored them, as he usually did, and soon enough they went back to talking/bickering amongst themselves.

Aye, he was looking forward to what the lass would do next. For him, that was foreign emotion to him to be sure, especially these days, but he found he was looking forward to it nonetheless.

The red coals in the fire had turned black by the time I was finished my bath. Bracing myself on the rim of the tub, I pulled my pruned reddened body from the now tepid water. Immediately my nipples hardened into tight buds from the contrast in temperature. Water dripped onto the cold stones under my feet as I used a small dishtowel sized piece of cloth to wipe the excess water from my body. Shivering, I pulled on the gown he was kind enough to leave out for me to wear, or so he told me as he was leaving. At least it was clean, but it made me wonder who in the hell it had actually belonged to.

After I gave myself a headache wondering how any of this was possible, I climbed down on the floor and tugged a smelly fur over my shoulders, trying to keep the chill at bay. I was almost asleep when I heard the door scrape against stone. My body tensed immediately.

A few moments later, the door scraped shut once more as the heavy clank of metal sounded in the darkness as the bolt was brought down into place.

"Lass, are ye asleep?" Heavy footsteps thudded on the stones as they drew nearer to my makeshift bed on the floor.

Feigning sleep, I squeezed my eyes tightly shut.

I felt, rather than saw, him standing over me. My heart pounded a mile a minute, drowning out everything else. I held my breath, wondering if he could hear it too.

When I was almost out of air, he mumbled some kind of expletive and shuffled back across the room. I gasped for breath as the bed creaked and two distinct thuds hit the floor. More things dropped with a swishing sound and then the bed creaked louder. He emitted a rather loud groan as more swishing and a final creak, sounded.

"Good night to ye, lass," he said so low I wasn't sure if I had heard him or if it was wishful thinking on my part. Either way, the room became quiet. As my eyes drifted shut, the quiet was broken as he started to snore. It started out as a low rumble, at first, but grew in volume as the night progressed. Shoving the fur over my head to buffer the sound, I finally, albeit reluctantly, drifted off to sleep.

CHAPTER SEVEN

Gavin stood over her sleeping form, watching the rise and fall of her chest and the way her full lips parted slightly, expelling her breath. Irritation filled him. He swiped his hand over his face and pushed his hair back over his shoulder. Why he was irritated was not something he wanted to ponder overmuch, but it may have had something to do with the fact that when he mentioned her tending him in bed, she didn't seem overly enthusiastic at the prospect. Women normally fought for his attention and all too willingly fell into his arms without the slightest provocation on his part. Granted, that had not happened for a while since he had recently escaped the hangman's noose but it had happened before, quite often.

Now however, that he was a wanted man, as were the other men with him, there were '13' of them in total and they were damned. So when the King had commandeered them from their fate, which was to die for a paltry misdeed or two and in some cases three, they had all readily accepted the reprieve he had offered them. But he had yet to do what was asked of him and instead of slaying the monster of Loch Morar, and in doing so retrieve the treasure; he was now awaiting the Kings retribution, as one would await the other shoe to drop.

The other problem was that he also needed to feed his men, so they had resorted to stealing, which was another crime punishable by death. He only just missed the hangman's noose only to be a candidate for the gallows once again if he was ever caught.

I was dreaming and it was a rather good dream too. This dream was filled with '13' handsome Highlanders and one in particular that set my heart to pounding. The sun heated my face and I rolled over slowly, enjoying the warmth from it. Something pushed against my arm. I cracked my eyes open only to find a filthy boot beside my hand. My eyes slowly climbed up from the boot to a bare leg, then climbing higher, up a muscular body to the same blue-green eyes of the man I had been having the heated dream about.

Scrambling up to sitting, I pushed my hair from my face. It would seem I wasn't dreaming after all. "Good morning." I rubbed my eyes.

"What's good about it?" he snapped.

I tensed from his tone. "Looks like someone woke up from the wrong side of bed," I mumbled.

"Lass, ye need to speak clearly if ye want me ta answer ye. I cannot understand ye with all the mumbling ye always do, aye?"

"Oh, so, Mister, aye, och, and ye, is complaining about my speech?" *Really?* As if. I was only half way through one of my staple eye rolls when his expression changed and not in a good way.

"Och," he exhaled as a fierce frown pulled his dark brows together. "If I were ye I'd watch that sharp tongue of yers, lass, if ye want to keep it in yer mouth."

Wait…what? Was he kidding or threatening me? Just to be safe I swallowed back my snappy retort.

"The morning is waning, and we need to break our fast before we leave."

"Well, don't let me stop you."

His frown turned even more severe which I didn't think was possible. "Ye are the one that will be making the food ta break our fast, so if I were ye I would get moving."

"How dare you." I stood up, and the top of my head barely reached his shoulder.

"How dare I what?" His brows nearly covered his eyes, as he stared me down— again, not in a good way.

I may not understand everything he was saying but his expression alone made me hold my aforementioned tongue. "Okay."

"Once ye rouse yerself and do yer morning ablutions' ye will need ta go down ta the cook room and prepare our meal so we may break our fast."

I wanted to break something, all right, but it had nothing to do with food. "Sure."

His scowl softened significantly but I still held my tongue. "There is water behind the screen." And with that, he turned on his heel and left the room before I could even respond.

After his hasty exit, I did rouse myself (his words) not mine and went behind the screen to relieve myself. There was a bowl with water and I splashed some on my face. Exhausted from lack of sleep; not to mention the firm dressing down I had just received for God only knows what reason, and after I made myself reasonably presentable I made my way through the darkened corridors and down the steep stairs, heading off in the direction I presumed the cook room to be. Surprisingly, I had only taken two wrong turns before I finally found it.

A good hour or more had passed before I could figure out how to cook something that slightly resembled food in a big black pot hanging over the fire. Granted I had cooked in a cast iron skillet on camping trips with my ex, but nothing like this. This was ridiculous.

Straightening up, I pressed my hands against my aching back, purveying my attempt at making breakfast. Food on a whole was on the slim side here. So I made do with what looked like oats and made my version of Oatmeal, which didn't look that appetizing. It may have had something to do the burnt bits of brown floating on the top and throughout the unappetizing concoction. And even though I made it, I was reluctant to taste it. There was no meat, either.

There was something, however, that looked like an old piece of shoe leather on the rough-wood-work table. I supposed was some archaic version of bacon, however, I had no idea how to cook it or even cut it.

The kitchen, which was more of a dingy room with blackened stone walls from smoke and one tiny window that barely let any light inside didn't have much in the way of utensils other than a few spoons, which looked a bit too modern and I couldn't help wondering if this was something brought from the future as well. If it was, they should have sent pans, food, and some damn decent clothing to wear. The dress was scratchy and had a strange odor clinging to it. There were some dried herbs but since I had no idea what they were so I didn't want to chance using them in the food.

A rather large dog sat in the corner and watched my every move. It looked like it had mange since part of the fur was missing in spots and it also looked hungry. Using a long-handled wooden spoon, I dipped it into the pot and scooped up some of the 'Oatmeal Surprise' I made. The food stuck to the spoon like glue.

With a hefty shake, I shook it off on the floor.

The dog walked over to it, sniffed, made a whining noise, and then with his tail tucked between his legs he ran straight out the open door.

Good lord. If the dog ran from my food, what the heck were all those men going to do?

"What is taking her so long?" Callum complained, rubbing his empty belly.

"I do not think she knows how ta cook." Muir reached up and scratched his head.

"What did we get rid of the crone for? At least she could cook."

"Aye, but she wasn't much ta look at."

"Who cares if she was comely, at least she could cook and look, we are now going ta starve."

"The lass doesn't have much to work with, remember?" Muir added.

"Aye, I remember." Callum adjusted his bottom on the chair, leaned forward and placed his elbows on the table awaiting his meal.

Gavin massaged his forehead as he listened to his men moan like a bunch of hens. He was hungry too but he knew there was not much in the larder to cook. He felt bad for being so short with the lass earlier, but he was not sure what to do about her or the treasure he needed to retrieve. So he had taken his foul mood out on the lass. He decided, he would make it up to her, at least he hoped he might, but he wouldn't make any promises.

As I entered the hall, thirteen hungry pairs of eyes tracked my every move. I dropped the pot on the table. The wood bowed underneath the weight. I wiped my sweating hands on my skirt and stepped back.

"Come and get it," I called as loudly as I could and then took another deliberate step away as the young man I remembered from last night stood and walked over toward the pot.

"Och, lass." His lip curled in displeasure. "What is that?" He pointed down at the pot.

"It's 'Oatmeal Surprise'," I informed him none too nicely, since I was tired and grumpy.

His brow creased as he leaned forward and took a good sniff. Leaning back, he shook his head morosely. "What are the wee bits of brown in there?" He pointed down at the pot again.

"That's the surprise." I took another step backward, looking for an exit.

"Can ye tell me what it is?" His eyes, I noticed, were the exact shade of blue-green as my Highlander, err, roomie, and couldn't help but wonder if they were related.

"No…" I shook my head adamantly back and forth. "That would ruin the surprise."

Eyes filled with horror landed on mine. "I thank ye for yer trouble lass, but if it's all the same ta ye, I think I would like ye ta make me something else ta eat."

"Well too bad," I nearly yelled. "That's all there is. Take it or leave it." There was no way in hell I was going to make more food. This was hard enough to make and besides, I wasn't lying, there really wasn't anything else to eat. At least nothing I could identify.

A squeamish look crossed the young man's face as he lifted up a bowl from the table. Reaching out, he grabbed the wooden spoon and pulled. It didn't move. Setting his bowl down, he tried again. This time he used two hands. Finally, the spoon came out making much the same noise as my body did when I was extracted from the mud yesterday. He whopped the spoon on the edge of the bowl and a rather sickly sounding plop of oatmeal made its way down inside.

"Thank ye," he murmured and stepped back away from the pot with a cross between curiosity and horror on his face at the prospect of eating what he had just scooped up.

After that, the rest of the men, who all looked to be in their late teens or early twenties, lined up with similar wooden bowls as they took turns fighting with the spoon until they too had a bowlful of the disgusting meal I made. I didn't blame them for the looks they were giving the food, as it too, made me wrinkle my face in disgust and I was the one who cooked it. Last but certainly not least, the laird, Gavin, my grumpy roomie, came to stand beside me. "Lass, is this the best ye could do?"

"Yes," I nearly cried. "I tried, I really did."

"I am sure ye did," his tone softened. "I didn't give ye much ta work with, now did I?"

"No, you did not."

"I apologize, but that is all I have."

Fighting back tears, I sniffed. I wasn't sure if they were from relief or exhaustion, maybe both. "I really did try."

"I can see that, lass." He too lifted his bowl, finally, and scraped a bit of my 'Oatmeal Surprise'

out of the pot. He slapped the spoon on the side of his bowl and it made a gross sounding plop when it finally released down into his bowl. "Thank ye, for yer efforts, lass."

"You're welcome." I sniffed again and wiped away my tears with the back of my sleeve.

"Ye may have some as well, lass." He stepped out of my way so I could get to the pot.

I did not want to eat...*that*... but as I stood there, thirteen pairs of eyes turned on me...with spoons poised... waiting.

"Great," I fake enthused and lifted up a bowl. I grabbed the spoon but it was even worse than earlier. It was stuck well and good. Setting my bowl down, using both hands, I tried again and scraped a miniscule amount of food off the bottom of the pot. My scoop had a lot more bits of brown and black than the others.

Holding one hand on my bowl, I smacked the spoon down on the other side.

Nothing happened.

It did not go unnoticed to me that my audience of thirteen still had not taken a bite of their food.

No, instead, they were watching me with rapt interest. A flash of irritation shot through me and I really slammed the spoon down on my bowl. A glop of the slop finally released from the spoon and landed inside. Giving them a sheepish grin, I made my way over to the corner of the room where the only empty chair stood. All eyes were still trained on me. Faking my exuberance, I shoved my spoon in my bowl and took a bite. I immediately felt like spitting it back out but couldn't since everyone was watching me. I swallowed and made an "*Hmmm, mmm,*" sound and then once everyone was turned back to their bowls of food, I pressed my hand to my mouth so I didn't spit it back out. Literally forcing myself, I swallowed the most disgusting thing I had ever eaten and that was saying something since I accidentally ate a bug once.

"Muir," Callum said, keeping his voice low turning his attention back to his food. "If this..."

he pointed down to his bowl, "is what we will have ta break our fast for the next week, I want ye to know I will stick ta my word and ye can have all my second helpings."

Muir made a snorting noise. "Callum, if this is what we are eating for the next week, I want no parts of yer second helpings, let alone my first helpings. Besides, it doesn't look like there is enough for any second helpings."

"Och, Muir! That is no way ta act after the lass has went ta all the trouble to make food for ye."

"If ye think it is so great, by all means, ye can have my first helpings as well."

Callum made a face. "What are the crunchy brown bits, do ye suppose?" He took a bite.

"Bugs."

Callum gagged. "Och, Muir…" he choked.

Muir laughed and took a bite of his food. He too, gagged as he tried to swallow.

Now it was Callum's turn to laugh, that is, until one of the brown bits in his bowl moved. Then his laughter turned quickly back into a gagging fit.

Gavin eyed his men, noting the green expressions on their faces as they dutifully ate their paltry meal and then turned his attention back to the lass, who also looked a bit green. His belly grumbled. Throwing caution to the wind, he took a bite of his own food and he too, thought he might very well be sick. This, what he was eating, wouldn't be fit for a dog, let alone his starving men. He needed to get some real food soon or at this rate they would surely starve.

CHAPTER EIGHT

reakfast ended quickly. Each of the men were kind enough to thank me for the meal and then they vacated the premises, promptly taking themselves out of the castle, all looking a little greener than they had before they started the meal. Now the only one remaining was my grumpy roomie, the Laird. He said nary a word but simply watched me from across the room.

It was a bit unsettling to say the least. Finally, I couldn't take him watching me any longer. Standing, I carried my bowl to the table and set it down. Busying myself, I gathered up the other spoons, once again noticing they looked like they were from the future, not the past like they should and the bowls to wash. As I placed them on top of one another I noticed they still had most of my 'Oatmeal Surprise' still inside. I couldn't blame them. My own bowl was still pretty full as well.

"Lass," Gavin said.

I looked up and my breath caught as I looked at his handsome face. "Yes," I somehow managed to answer.

"Thank ye for the meal."

"Oh, don't mention it." I waved my hand dismissively in the air.

"Ye don't cook much, do ye?"

I set the stack of bowls down which made a resounding thud on the table. "No, I don't."

"Didn't the crone, err, gypsy, ask ye if ye could cook?"

"Not really."

He nodded his head, seemingly accepting my answer. "We don't have much food in the larder."

"I know." He was slouched back in the chair with his long legs kicked out in the front. It was hard not to stare.

"We...I mean, I," he amended, and sat forward, "will try to get ye something better ta cook with in the future."

"I just don't know what half of that stuff is..." I tried to explain.

"Aye, I suppose ye do not." He exhaled and stood up from the table. "What do ye usually eat?"

"Spaghetti, Alfredo, Lobster on special occasions..." I stopped talking because his eyes were rounding. "Right," I sighed and rubbed my sweaty palms on my dress. "You don't know what I am talking about do you?"

He shook his head. "Nay, lass, I do not."

"Well, it's really good and easy to make..." I stopped again because his eyes were growing larger by the moment and not in a 'Wow...that sounds delicious way'. "All righty then..."

"Did ye bring such wonders from the future with ye?" he asked with a hopeful gleam in his eyes...or was that merely hunger?

"No, well, I am not sure. The gypsy, err, woman, did give me a basket."

The hopeful gleam was back in his sexy eyes. "Where is it?"

"I don't know." I lifted my shoulders in a noncommittal shrug.

He raked his hand through his dark hair, in aggravation, I supposed, and expelled a lengthy breath. "Then I will have to leave for a while," he said as though coming to some kind of decision.

"Wait...what?" I stepped closer to him, and was once again reminded of how large he really was in comparison to me.

"I will have to leave ye for a wee bit." He stared down at me with a curious look on his handsome face.

"Why?" My heart rate jumped into double time. I didn't want him to leave me... alone. "Where will the rest of the, ah, men, be?"

"No need ta fear, lass, they will be coming with me."

I wasn't necessarily afraid of them being here with me but the opposite. I didn't want to be here all alone.

"I need ta find some food for us ta eat."

That was true enough, I supposed, but what was I going to do while he and the other men were gone. As if sensing my distress, he added, "Ye can clean up this...while we are away." He swept his hand through the air indicating the hall.

"Clean what exactly?"

He lifted his brows. "This..." Again he indicated the room we were in.

I looked around at the mess. "By myself?"

"Do ye see someone I do not?" His brow lifted again.

"Well no..."

"Then ye have yer answer, aye?"

"Where do you keep your cleaning supplies?"

"My what?" His brows creased.

"Oh, never mind." What was the point? The man obviously had no idea what I was talking about.

He gave me another one of his curious looks.

"Do you have anything in particular you would like me to do, other than clean this..." Dump, I wanted to say, but instead swept my hand in the air, not able to keep the derision from my voice.

"Do ye need more duties while I am away?"

"No...not at all." I didn't even want to do this.

"Ye bit off a bit more than ye could chew, didn't ye, lass?"

I sighed. "I suppose."

"Not ta worry, lass, there is plenty ta keep ye busy."

"I can see that."

He chuckled and took a step closer. Again my belly did another involuntary flutter.

"I will be back before ye know it, lass." He was standing so close my temperature immediately shot upward. "And if ye are good..." Lifting his hand, he cupped my face tenderly, his thumb caressing the side of my jaw. I had all I could do not to press my face closer to his hand. "I will even consider letting ye tend ta me later." He gave me a winning smile that made my breath hitch and my toes curl in my shoes.

"Oh, joy! Not!" I said callously without thinking what I was really saying. It was more of a knee-jerk reaction because I was so flustered and didn't know how to respond.

His smile turned upside down into a severe frown as his dark brows drew together and that pained look I had seen briefly earlier entered his eyes for a moment before it was replaced with a cold unnerving stare. I shivered in spite of the warmth I felt standing so close to him.

"Do not forget ta change the rushes." He turned on his heel and stormed out of the castle.

"I didn't mean…" I tried to explain, but it was too late, he was already gone.

"Way to go, Paige! Of all the stupid, idiotic things to say..." I stomped around, feeling like a real 'b'. I didn't know what I was thinking. I didn't mean it the way it sounded. And obviously, he didn't know I was being sarcastic because of how embarrassed I was and now he probably thought I was...well, I didn't know, but he wasn't happy, that was for sure. And neither was I. When I asked for a Highlander for my own I didn't stop to consider the repercussions of such a wish. I certainly didn't think I would be made to do menial labor for my wished highlander as well.

Fifteen minutes later, after I had a mini tantrum, where I railed to myself and stomped my feet around the filthy hall expelling a good amount of my energy, I decided to just do as he asked.

Surprisingly, not only was cleaning universal, it also spanned time, with the exception of vacuums, dusters, and well, the products I needed to clean with.

However, I somehow made do with what I had. I boiled water in the pot over the fire in the kitchen and once it was good and hot, I dumped the bowls inside as well as the spoons to get rid of the sticky remnants of my 'Oatmeal Surprise'. While that was boiling away, I cleaned up the rest of the kitchen as best as I could by wiping down the table and putting things away on the shelves.

Now, I was back in the main hall with nothing but dirty grass all over the floor that looked like hay. Not able to find a broom, I tried kicking it. Dust floated up in the air, choking me. Covering my mouth, I backed away from the cloud.

"There's got to be an easier way."

In hopes of finding a broom, I ran back to the kitchen/cook room. No luck.

"Think, Paige..." I walked in circles and then finally came up with an idea. Leaving the kitchen, I walked out the back door. It was the same one the dog ran out of earlier. A rather bushy pine tree with low hanging branches was off to the side of the dirt pathway. Walking over to it, I broke off one of the smaller limbs.

"This should do the trick."

With my makeshift broom in hand, I made my way back to the great hall. Swishing it back and forth, I tried sweeping. Again, dust floated up in the air and some large chunks of something that looked a lot like bones went sailing across the room and pinged against the stone wall.

"Gross."

I closed my eyes, not wanting to see what it was. At least the pine-branch was better than kicking the hay/rushes but it didn't help with the cloud of dust. What I needed was a cloth for my face. Since I didn't see anything else to use, I lifted my gown and pulled up the bottom of the linen under-dress and ripped off the ruffle and then tied it around my face. If I had a mirror I was sure I would look like a bank robber.

Getting to work, I swept/kicked and dragged the smelly grass/hay out the door. With one big push, I shoved the entire pile over the side of the stairs, where they fell into a heap. No one was around save for the mangy dog, the one that had run from my food earlier, and his head was going back and forth like he was watching a tennis match as I made each trip outside until I finished sweeping out the main hall.

Standing my broom in the corner, I looked around at my handiwork. It *did* look better and it definitely smelled better too. Brushing off my hands, I made my way back to the kitchen.

I checked the dishes in the pot. Most of the water was gone. Lifting the hem of my gown up, I wrapped it around my hands and pulled the pot off the hook and set it down on the table. Once the water cooled, I pulled out the now reasonably clean dishes to dry on a large piece of cloth.

Twenty minutes later, after I finished with the dishes, I went back to the main hall to see what else needed cleaning. All in all, the place looked pretty good and if I wasn't so damn tired I would have patted myself on my back for achieving that no small feat in just a single day. Walking over to the door, I looked outside. The sun was gradually fading from the horizon as heavy clouds gathered, pressing down from the skies above. It looked like a storm was brewing and now that I had stopped moving I realized how alone I was. Shivering, I rubbed my arms.

A large tree in the center of the yard shook in the wind as dust and debris lifted in the air pushing its way across the flattened grass and out the open gates. The fine hairs on the back of my neck stood on end as an uneasy feeling coursed through me.

I felt like someone was watching me.

Slowly, I turned to look over my shoulder but the gloomy hall was just as empty as I had left it.

Not wanting to go back inside, I sat down on the stairs and waited for my highlander, correction, highlanders, to come back.

CHAPTER NINE

"Come now, Shamus," Gavin said in a placating tone with his hands held aloft as he was rounded on by the large tavern owner who was wielding a pitchfork at him.

"Och, ye know we are in a bad way what with the drought and all the wee bairns the misses and me daughters keep popping out at every turn."

"Aye, I know," Gavin sighed. He scrubbed his hands over his face, and let them drop back down to his sides. His men kept back, like he instructed, watching. They were only to interfere if he needed them and Shamus, even though he was a large man and carried on with a good amount of bluster, his threats were just that, threats. He would not act on them.

"Gavin, ye are my friend and ye know I would help if I could."

"Aye, I know."

"I know yer intentions are good, but ye have yet ta give me back what ye borrowed that last time ye were here."

"I would if I could, ye know that. And when I get the treasure…"

"Ye keep talking about this supposed treasure but ye still have not found it have ye?

"Well, no, not yet but…" He wasn't going to tell the man the deal he made with the latest witch. The villagers were a superstitious lot. If he told him about the lass he had at the castle who claimed to be from the future, either Shamus would think him crazy or he might gather the village folk to come to the castle to have a look for themselves. The way Paige talked and looked, even though she was dressed in his colors the villagers would immediately realize something was not quite right. Then they would get scared and do to her what they always did when they didn't understand something.

They would try to burn her at the stake like the one before the last. And when that didn't work, they would drown her in the nearest body of water, which was his Loch to see if she would float. And she did; instead of releasing her, they weighed her down with rocks to make sure she did not come back, which she didn't.

Nay. He'd seen enough of that kind of barbaric behavior to last a lifetime. He wouldn't want that fate on the lass, even if she was a true witch. He would need to talk to her again, see if the crone told her how to go about getting the treasure from the monster without being used as a sacrifice.

Shamus exhaled and stuck his pitchfork in the dirt. "I can give ye some eggs, a few vegetables from the larder and a few kegs of ale."

"Nay, I don't want to take the last of yer eggs or vegetables. He left the ale part out."

"It's fine," he said. "We can spare a few."

"I thank ye kindly for yer generous nature, Shamus."

"Just remember the service I have done for ye, if and or when ye ever find that damnable treasure, aye?"

"I will not forget."

"Tilly, fetch the Laird his bounty."

"Aye father," said a young pretty girl not more than ten and six with curling red hair. She gave Gavin a small smile before she ducked back into the tavern behind her father to do his bidding.

"Now," Shamus said, holding his massive arm out. "Let's get a drink and ye can tell me what ye have been about since the last I laid eyes on ye."

Gavin nodded his head at his men letting them know to keep an eye out and followed Shamus inside the darkened tavern.

"This tastes a lot better than our breakfast," Callum noted as he took the last bite of his stew and finished off the rest of the ale in his tankard.

"Aye, it does." Muir lifted his own cup and finished off the contents, then set his cup back down and wiped his mouth with his sleeve.

The rest of the men sat around on benches or the ground beneath a tree, eating and drinking as well. They were talking jovially amongst themselves as they waited the return of their laird.

"What do ye think the lass has gotten into whilst we have been away?"

Muir shrugged. "I heard the laird tell her ta clean the castle."

"Och, I do not envy the lass that task."

"Me neither," said Muir.

"Do ye think she is hungry?"

"Nay, there was plenty of the rotten breakfast left. She can eat that if she gets too hungry."

Callum made a face at the mention of their terrible breakfast. "Mayhap we should bring her some stew?"

"Ye can give her yers," he said. "I already ate mine."

"Aye, I did too," Callum said, eyeing his now empty bowl.

CHAPTER TEN

The sun had faded into the horizon and fat bellied clouds pressed down from the skies above when Gavin finally stepped back out of the pub. Feeling no pain as he was well into his cups, he grasped the door. Unsteady on his feet, he made his way over to his horse.

Standing, his men handed back the tankards and the bowls from the stew they were fed and then remounted their own horses one by one, reining them around.

"Thank ye Shamus," Gavin said. "I will not forget the generosity ye have shown me and my men."

"I will expect ye ta pay me back with interest when ye find this elusive treasure, aye?"

"Aye, I give ye my word." Gavin swung up into his saddle. His horse danced sideways ready to be on his way.

"See that ye stick ta it," Shamus called out.

"Aye, I will," he promised.

Once his men said their farewells to all of Shamus' daughters who were enthusiastically waving, he reined his horse around.

They had a goodly amount of food that would stave off their hunger for a bit longer. He only hoped the lass knew how to cook it. Luckily, a few of his men were busy while he was talking with Shamus and had somehow gotten two rabbits to add to their bounty along with a chicken.

Fat droplets of rain splattered down from the heavens above as they drunkenly headed back towards the castle.

One highlander slipped away from the rest and made his way back toward the tavern.

CHAPTER ELEVEN

With the heavy clouds pressing down and with the sun now being gone, it was almost completely dark.

"Please don't rain." I wasn't too keen on storms and was hoping against hope the storm would pass but I wasn't to be that lucky. One fat drop landed on my head, then two, and then a bucket of drops rained down on me, forcing me back inside the castle into the dim hall.

Shadows stretched across the room, and the fire was almost out. I stood in the doorway watching the rain bounce down on the ground and create small rivers in the dirt. Pitch forks of lighting streaked down from the sky and the Earth shook as the thunder rolled. The wind picked up, pushing the heavy sheets of rain inside from the torrential downpour, until I finally had to shut myself inside the castle. Shaking off the rain, I made my way to the fireplace, bent down, and tossed on a few more logs. The flames licked up the sides of the wood, and burned brightly once more. Standing, I wiped my hands on my gown and pulled a chair over in front of the fire, then another one to prop my feet on.

Once again I had the feeling someone was watching me. My heartbeat broke into a gallop as I turned but all that greeted me were shadows from the flames shifting across the now clean floor. Rubbing my arms, I situated myself back on the chairs and stared into the fire as I tried to figure out what I was going to do.

I was tired and even though I had a rather delectable Highlander to look at, I knew at some point I would need to get the hell outta dodge, but how? Now that was the million-dollar question. There had to be a way though. The damned lying gypsy made her way out of here and tricked me into coming here in her place. Was it some kind of witchery, or was some other magical conduit used? Sure I was reaching, but what else was there to consider? I didn't know.

The warmth from the fire, along with exhaustion from cleaning all day, had my eyes drifting closed. Every so often, I would jerk awake when another spike of lightening lit up the room or a roll of thunder shook the castle.

"Where are they?" I gathered my arms around myself and hunkered down more in my chair.

My eyes had just drifted shut again when I heard a scratching sound. Jerking upright, I dropped my feet from the chair and spun around. My skin prickled but I didn't see anything. God, I hoped it wasn't a rat. Or worse, some other God-awful thing I had no knowledge of from the past.

"Just your imagination, Paige," I said trying to calm my growing unease and stop my rampant fear from gaining momentum.

Lifting my feet once again, I propped them up on the chair. I had nearly convinced myself I was imagining the noise when I heard it again. This time I was sure it was coming from the door. Jumping from the chair, I warily made my way across the room, and pressed my ear against the rough wood.

Again, I heard the scratching sound. Stupidity reared its ugly head and I did something I would never do at home if I heard a noise outside my door. I grasped hold of the handle, telling myself I would only take a peek. Maybe my Highlanders had forgotten their keys. I snorted in derision as a bubble of hysteria broke from my throat. *There was no lock on the door, so there would be no need for a key*, the sane part of my mind ranted at me. Still, I pulled open the door and immediately screamed.

CHAPTER TWELVE

The mangy dog from earlier unceremoniously shoved his way through the door and bounded past me in a dripping ball of fur into the hall. Removing my trembling hand from my chest, I shut the door.

The dog shook his body and splattered water all over the floor I had tried so hard to clean.

"Nice doggy." I took a step forward with my hand outstretched to pat its massive head, glad to have some company.

Instead of wagging its tail, happy that I saved him from the storm, he got into a defensive stance and bared its teeth at me, growling low in its throat. What was left of the fur rose up into hackles on its back. Of course, it couldn't be a nice little dog that I let in. No, instead it was a massive pony sized one.

Once again, my heartbeat broke into a gallop that soon turned into a dead run as the dog closed the space between us. Taking a tentative step back, I kept my gaze on the dog, heading slowly for the stairs. I knew if I broke into a run he would attack me. I'd watched enough survival shows to know that much. Lot of good it did me though, because I usually got bored and turned off the television before I found out how the people got away. Each step I took backward... the dog took a step forward.

I tried to control my breathing, I didn't want it to sense my fear, but damn, how did one not act terrified of a dog that could easily rip a person in two with just one snap from its mouth that was filled with rather sharp gruesome teeth.

Maybe it's giving you some payback for trying to feed it your 'Oatmeal Surprise' my sick mind chided me as I took another step backward. I was now on the stairs, but I could tell the dog was growing impatient. It may have had something to do with the fact that it was growling even more with each step I took as I tried to distance myself from him.

"Nice doggy," I said again, trying to keep my voice level and calm as I took another step upward.

I wished I had something to throw to distract him, like a steak or a bone, but of course, I had none of those things. Then I remembered I did have shoes. Didn't dogs like eating shoes? I couldn't remember. It would work, I thought, at least I hoped it would. Reaching down slowly, I pulled on one of my shoes.

The dog took two steps forward as I fought to release my damn shoe. It finally gave but my time was up. The dog was poised for attack.

"Fetch," I yelled as loud as my constricted throat would allow and threw the shoe as hard as I could. My shoe crashed against the far wall with a resounding thwap.

The dog emitted a fierce growl and swung its head in the direction I threw my shoe. I didn't wait to find out if he was going to chase after it. I took off up the rest of the stairs. I could hear the dog spinning around on the stone trying to gain traction with its nails as I sprinted like a seasoned athlete with my skirts held high and only one shoe on my foot down the dark corridor to his room. I just made it inside when the barking grew in volume and I knew he was just inches away from gaining on me. I was done for.

By the grace of God, I was able to slam the door shut as the dog slid into it, barking, and scratching the wood with its paws. In the distance, I could swear I heard cackling laughter that sounded a lot like the gypsy that sent me here, but that wasn't possible. Must be hearing things, I thought.

Heart pounding, I brought the bolt home and pressed myself against the wood, trying to get my breathing under control. The dog started whining and scratching the door more.

"Shut the hell up," I railed, clearly having lost the tenuous hold on what was left of my control.

The dog whimpered one last time and then miraculously shut up. It sounded as though it had left but I didn't care. There was no way in hell I was going to leave the safety of this room, no matter what.

On cue, my belly grumbled. Reminding me, I hadn't eaten anything since the gross 'Oatmeal Surprise' I made. "Well, too damn bad," I told my growling stomach. "You will just have to starve.

Crossing over to the fireplace, I put some more logs on the dying embers and coaxed the fire back to life. Standing once more, I walked over behind the screen to relieve myself and then cleaned up as best as I could with the leftover water I used this morning.

After I finished, I decided a little snooping wouldn't be out of order. I looked around at his things. He had some paper on the table as well as an inkwell but nothing written down. Losing interest, I made my way to his chest and tried to open it, but it was locked.

"Dangit!" I kicked the trunk with my shoeless foot and was rewarded by a sharp pain shooting up through my big toe, which put an abrupt end to my snooping.

Not having anything else to do, I threw some more wood on the fire, paced the room a few times and then sat on the fur on the floor, thinking I should just go to sleep and maybe while I was asleep my Highlander, err, Highlanders, might return.

Lying down, I tried to get comfortable, but it was cold and the floor was hard. Shivering, I sat up again. Looking over my shoulder, my eyes drifted to his rather large comfy looking bed.

"Why not," I said. Not seeing the harm in it, I stood up, walked across the room and pulled back the furs on top of his bed. I wasn't even the least bit surprised to see he had very modern sheets on his bed as well as pillows. I sat down on the edge and kicked my feet out on top.

"Wow."

It felt like I was in a bed in a five-star hotel, compared to the scrap of filth he had me sleeping on the night before.

Making up my mind, I climbed from the bed and crossed over to the door. I undid the latch just as another roll of thunder shook the room along with a flash of lighting. My feet barely hit the floor as I ran back to the safety of his bed. Sitting back down, I kicked off my remaining shoe, torn sock and climbed under the furs to the point I was buried. I made a little air hole for myself but other than that there were no visible parts of my body showing. I decided I would get some much needed sleep and since I was a light sleeper, when I heard him come back, I would get up before he even made it to his room, or so I told myself.

CHAPTER THIRTEEN

The '13' Highlanders made their way back into the main hall of the castle. Each of the men were drenched and chilled to the bone.

"Put the supplies away in the larder and get some rest," Gavin told his men as he made his way to the stairs.

"Och, why is the floor so wet?" asked Callum, sidestepping a rather large puddle in the middle of the room.

Muir shrugged. "At least it smells clean."

"Aye, that it does," said Alec, as he unhooked his plaid and laid it over the chair in front of the fire to dry.

"The lass may not be able to cook but she can obviously clean," Graham noted as he twisted the length of his hair which released more water on the floor.

Gavin wiped the water from his face with his plaid, and looked around the hall, not believing his eyes. It was clean. Well, as clean as could be expected, he supposed. He also noticed the rushes were gone and decided very quickly that was not such a bad thing since it smelled a lot better now. Feeling a sense of urgency to see the lass, to make sure she was all right, or so he told himself, he took the stairs two at a time to his chamber.

At once, he noticed the dog curled up outside his door. The dog lifted his massive head and then seeing who was coming down the hall, dropped it back down to the floor. Gavin stepped around the dog, and opened his door. It scraped open against the stone barely making any sound this time. His eyes went to the place in front of the fire and his heart dropped at what he saw. She wasn't here.

For some reason, unbeknownst to hi, his heart sped up. He tore out of his room, back down the stairs to the hall. A few of the men had yet to retire to their sleeping quarters. "Where is she?" he nearly yelled.

Callum started, stifling a yawn. "Who?"

"The lass?"

"Do ye suppose she left?"

"Why would she leave?" Gavin asked more to himself than the remaining men in the room.

"Mayhap, she didn't want to clean for ye anymore," Muir added helpfully.

Graham stood up from the chair. "Mayhap something happened to her?" He bent over and picked up a lone shoe. "Is this hers?"

Gavin's belly twisted involuntarily at the sight. Why would her shoe be down here? Did she leave, just as Callum had said or did something happen to her. Irritated more with himself than his men, he made his way to the cook room. Reaching the doorway, he pulled up short. The place was clean as well, at least cleaner than he had ever seen it. Walking over to the door, he opened it and peered through the blackness of the night.

The wind howled and water pelted against his body and his face as he tried to see some sign as to where she may have gone. He saw a figure move out from under a pine tree and relief filled him, until he saw who it was.

"What are ye doing out here?" Gavin watched as Broderick stepped out from under the pine tree.

"I was tending to the horses and got turned around in the storm."

Gavin merely nodded and pushed the door open wider so he could pass.

"Is something amiss?" Broderick asked.

"The lass, she is ..." He couldn't bring himself to say it. "Nothing."

Not having any answers readily available, he shut the door against the wind and rain. Turning around, he made his way back to the great hall.

After the long day and ride, not to mention the several tankards of ale he drank exhaustion was taking its toll, settling in against him. Barely able to keep his eyes open, he scrubbed his hands over his face and then dropped them to his sides. He hated to admit it, but he had been looking forward to seeing the lass, but apparently the feeling had not been mutual. Of course he knew it was his fault. Had he been kinder, mayhap she would have wanted to stay, for a bit at least. He'd run off the other one, Jillian, in much the same way he supposed. He had thought she was different though. He'd thought...well, it didn't matter anymore. She was gone now, just like Paige.

As he passed his men he ignored their questioning stares and made his way back to his chamber. An uneasy feeling settled in the pit of his stomach as he climbed the stairs and he decided it must have been from the stew he ate for there was no way the lass, one he barely knew, could make him feel thusly. Yes, it must have been something he ate souring his stomach. Not the lass. Or so he told himself.

Once inside his room, he brought the bolt home and undressed in front of the fire. He noticed the coals were still red as if someone had been tending it for most of the night but if the lass had truly left...a glimmer of hope filled him...he exhaled and shook his head.

What was the point?

Giving the fur on the floor a sidelong glance he made his way to his bed. With a heavy heart, he lifted the covers and climbed underneath.

He started when his feet hit something other than his mattress.

Jerking back the furs he looked down. The lass, his lass, he amended, was curled into a ball, hugging one of his pillows. Relief along with another emotion filled him and he decided it was one he didn't want to ponder overmuch, at least not now. Lifting his hand, he moved her hair from her face. She made the softest mewling sound in her sleep and squirmed closer to the warmth of his body. As he watched her, he decided he would let her sleep here tonight but on the morrow he fully intended to give her a firm dressing down, but even as he thought that, the corners of his lips lifted into one of his rare smiles.

Carefully, so as not to wake her, he pulled the furs back up to cover them both and then laid his head down next to hers on one of the pillows. Without thinking, he reached forward, gathered her sleeping form in his arms, and spooned her from behind as he drifted off into the most restful sleep he had in quite some time.

CHAPTER FOURTEEN

A dream...a most delicious, delectable dream...my foggy brain insisted as a warm calloused hand slid down inside my gown, covering my right breast and then gently caressed the peak of my rigid nipple. A pair of soft lips soon followed, accompanied by the rough scruff of beard against the top.

"Ye taste as sweet as honey, lass." A light stream of air whispered against my naked flesh and my body responded even though I was a little disappointed, because now I knew I was definitely dreaming. Every night, my dream Highlander gave me that very same line, soon followed by him telling me he was going to claim me for his verra own…

"I want ta taste ye," he murmured into my mouth, nibbling my lips as he slid down to my neck, trailing kisses down my throat.

My body tensed…*wait*…I didn't remember the *taste* part…

"I want to claim ye for my verra own, lass," he said gruffly, the sound coming from deep in his throat vibrated against my ear as though he was really with me, and not some delusion I conjured while I slept.

Definitely a dream.

Relaxing again, I let my sexy dream highlander have his way with my person.

Threading my hands into his long dark hair, I cradled his head to my breast as his lips kissed and his mouth sucked the sensitive skin.

Before I knew it, my dream Highlander's hand was under my gown, sliding further up my leg, to the warmth between my thighs.

A zing of pleasure shot through me as soon as his fingers touched the sensitive flesh, and even though I was sure I was dreaming, there was a small part of my brain sounding off a warning that said, maybe this felt a bit *too* real, a bit *too* good, but I chose to ignore it.

Fisting the sheets, my legs fell open a little wider as his fingers delved deeply inside, invading my body, and then pulling out, just enough, before sliding back inside again.

Every caress, every kiss, brought me closer to the edge and each time he bit my nipple, a bolt of pleasure shot through me. I felt pulled in a million different directions, his hands, his mouth, his body, all at once. I was awash in pleasure. With one last gentle stroke my entire body tensed, and before I knew it I was spiraling out of control, shattering from within against his hand.

CHAPTER FIFTEEN

Mortification set in the moment I felt the bed give beside me. After my explosive orgasm, I was pretty much ripped awake from the best dream I ever had only to realize I wasn't dreaming at all. That is when the mortification began to set in. Not only wasn't I dreaming, but a very real, very hot, Highlander, was lying on his back next to me. I knew this because I heard him breathing and felt the side of his warm body pressed against my own. Now that I remembered where I was and what I had just let a complete stranger do, I thought I just might die of embarrassment.

Thank the Lord it was dark.

The storm continued to rage outside and shake the walls of the castle.

Again, I felt him shift beside me and I thought I should say something, but I couldn't think of anything to say other than, *Wow, that was awesome*, but of course, I wouldn't say that. Even in my dream I had never thanked him (my dream Highlander) for doing all those wonderful things to my body. And now that I knew it had really happened, I was completely and unequivocally, mortified, and embarrassed, and of course so satiated that all I wanted to do was roll over and snuggle closer to him. As if reading my thoughts, he turned over on his side, wrapped his arm around my waist, and pulled me back against the length of his warm hard body once more.

In the darkness, as the storm rumbled and kicked up a good fuss outside, I waited for him to say something, anything… but as the minutes passed and his breathing became heavier, I had a feeling he wasn't going to say a word about what just happened without me prompting him to do so. Which, I wasn't, of course. Instead, I reveled in the way his muscular body felt pressed closely to mine and how his breath warmed the back of my neck and shoulder. Too soon, his breathing evened out and I felt the distinct rumbling from his chest as he began to snore.

Relaxing against him, now that he was sleeping once more, I felt torn. Part of me was glad for the reprieve. The other part of me however, the one that was apparently never satisfied, was a little upset he didn't say anything to me about what just happened between us. Who knew, maybe he wouldn't remember. Maybe if I got out of the bed, he would think it was all a dream and I wouldn't have to suffer through more embarrassment than was necessary for the duration of my stay, however long that may be. Now that I had that far-reaching thought in my mind, I made the hasty decision on what I had to do.

Carefully, so as not to wake him, I lifted his hand from my waist and reluctantly climbed from under the warmth of the furs. When my bare feet hit the hard, cold floor, I started second-guessing my decision to move. Garnering my resolve, I powered through it, and quickly made my way over to the smelly fur on the floor in front of the fire (my makeshift bed) and lay down on top.

Shivering, I twisted the fur around my body and as the storm continued to rage outside, I finally drifted off into a restless slumber.

Gavin slid his hand over to the now empty space at his side. He wasn't worried, though. She obviously only needed a moment of privacy. But when the minutes continued to tick by and she still did not come back to his bed, an all too familiar heaviness settled around his heart, reinforcing the wall that had started to crumble.

The storm had vanished by the time I woke and as I looked over at the now empty bed, it would seem, so had my highlander. My face heated as I remembered a bit too clearly what happened in that very same bed only a few short hours ago. Standing up, I hurriedly crossed the room to get ready for the day.

Once again, there was clean water in the basin and I splashed it on my face before washing up as best as I could. When I finished, I walked over in front of the fire, lifted the fur off the floor, and folded it into a nice square before placing it on the trunk. I made his bed as well. Fluffing the pillows more than needed, I tried to prolong the inevitable but my stomach grumbled loudly, reminding me I had yet to eat anything substantial since yesterday and that was almost too little food to even count. So even though I was being a chicken and didn't want to leave his room to face him in the light of day, my grumbling belly had other ideas.

So with one last look around, I left the room and made my way down the dark gloomy corridor, to the top of the stairs.

Much like the first night I was here, I stared down into the hall and was surprised to see it appeared empty save for the monstrous dog that was taking up residence in front of the damn door, sleeping.

Again my belly grumbled, spurring me to make a decision. Throwing caution to the wind, I very carefully and as quietly as I could, made my way down the stairs. The dog thankfully didn't move from its resting place. With my heart pounding too loudly, I gathered my skirts in my hand, preparing to make a break for the kitchen.

Taking off, I rounded the corner, and came to a skidding a halt. In the corner, where I could not see before, was a chair, and in that chair was my Highlander, and he was staring right at me. He didn't look happy. My breath caught in my throat as I waffled in place, not sure if I should run back to his room or face him and in doing so get this ridiculous humiliation business out of the way once and for all. So garnering my slipping resolve, I stayed where I was.

"Good morning," I called as cheerily as I could under the circumstances, albeit quieter than I normally would have due to the sleeping massive dog across the room.

He didn't move. Not a muscle and for a moment I didn't think he was going to say anything to me at all. On the verge of turning around and running back to his room, he finally spoke.

"Aye, it would seem some of us are having a good morning," he said in the sexy Scottish brogue of his that set my heart to pounding once more.

Uncrossing his long legs, he stood from the chair. As he approached me I was reminded of a panther, beautifully graceful but also deadly. I shivered in spite of the brave front I was putting on as he drew nearer.

"Och, lass," he sighed and stopped in front of me. "What am I ta do with ye?"

Anything you want, I almost blurted. "Whatever do you mean?" I squeaked out in a pitch too high, my voice betraying the calm façade' I was attempting to master but also obviously failing miserably by the look on his too handsome face.

A frown marred his perfect brow as he continued to stare me down. "Ye do not like it here much, do ye?"

"Well, I wouldn't say that," I attempted to sound breezy, not stupid and embarrassed like I felt.

His frown deepened as he lifted his hand to my face. My betraying body leaned towards his and I had all I could do to remain standing upright at the slightest touch from him. "Did ye sleep well?" His brow lifted a notch.

"Um..." He stroked his thumb across my jaw, which was doing a good job of distracting me from what I wanted to say.

"I can see that ye did, sleep well, that is. Aye?" His lips twitched upward and his eyes sparked with a mischievous gleam. The urge to lean forward, to place my hand on his beautiful face as he was mine was overwhelming and just as I was about to do something I would have kicked myself for later, he dropped his hand and stepped back away from me. Instinctively, I took a step forward, to what...chase after him? I wasn't sure, but whatever it was I forced myself to stop. My betraying eyes drifted back to his mouth, that very same mouth that had kissed me and...

"Well?"

"Huh?" I lifted my eyes back to his.

"Ah, lass, ye confuse me." He raked his hand through his hair, in exasperation I supposed.

"What do you find so confusing about me?"

"Ye run hot and cold. One moment ye are in my arms, writhing and mewling. Then after ye have yer fill from me, ye run away, scared, from the very thing that has given ye such pleasure."

My mouth popped open. I didn't know what to say to that. Since when were men so perceptive and blatantly candid? And to answer my own question, I would have said, never. I'd never met a man in my world like him but apparently things were a lot different here, in his world...in the past.

Just thinking that made a bubble of hysterical laughter slip from my mouth. Appalled, I covered my mouth but it was already too late. His expression turned on a dime and not in a good way.

"Lass," he exhaled, shaking his head. "I am getting a little tired of yer foolish games."

"Games?" I repeated.

"Aye..." His eyes were deadly serious.

In spite of the heat I felt with him near, my body involuntarily shivered.

"Tend ta yer chores, lass," he said as he turned to go.

"Wait," I called, feeling unsettled.

He stopped and turned towards me with an unreadable expression on his too handsome face as his brow slowly hitched up another notch.

I swallowed past the lump that had taken up residence in my throat. "What do you mean?"

"Which part?"

"Obviously, the game part," I deadpanned, being smart, partly because I was tired, and because I was nervous.

His eyes flashed with something akin to anger, making me shiver. "Ye need ta make up yer mind." And with that he turned on his heel, stalked across the hall and out the door.

Luckily, for me, the dog followed him out.

Shaking all over, I sat down in the chair he had vacated only moments before and rubbed my aching head. Now, I'd done it. I'd gone and made him angry...again.

"What are you doing, Paige?"

Of course, I didn't have an answer to my question any more than I had an answer to how I got here in the first place. And if I wasn't so damn hungry I probably would have gone straight back to his room and had a good lie down on the floor until I woke up in my own time. But as with most things I did, nothing was easy, so instead I stood up, and made my way to the kitchen to find something to eat.

After I ate some fresh fruit, a piece of bread and something that looked like beef jerky. I started on my daily chores which surprisingly didn't last as long as I would have thought. Once I was finished, I decided to go outside and see where all my highlanders had disappeared. Granted, there was only one highlander that I really cared to see but I included the others too so it would sound better. And it made me feel less pathetic, so I stuck with it.

As I stepped through the door, the sunlight instantly blinded me. Lifting my hand, I shielded my eyes. Since I had been inside the dim castle for most of the day doing my "chores" per my roomies, instructions, it took a few minutes for my eyes to adjust even though the sun was already slipping down from the sky. Wispy clouds floated past in stark contrast to the gray-blue backdrop of sky.

On the lookout for the dog, I made my way down the stairs. A cool breeze blew gently and made gooseflesh rise on my sweat-dampened skin. Leaves rustled on the branches of the only tree standing in the middle of the courtyard as the dirt under my feet made a slight crunching noise as I continued across the yard. A chicken was scratching the dirt and pecking at some unseen bug or grain as I passed by.

I had only made it a few feet when I had a distinct feeling that I was being watched again. It probably had more to do with my conscience than my prickling skin. Or so I thought until I turned around and saw a shadow slipping around the edge of the castle.

I took two steps forward, part of me thinking I should maybe follow it, but then another part of my mind, the sane part, said, "Hell No!"

For once, I let the voice of reason control me and went with the "Hell No!", and instead, walked in the other direction.

The sound of metal hitting metal drew me over across the yard, down a hill and past a low stone-wall with a gentle slope leading to a lower grassy field.

I rounded the corner my eyes widened at what I saw. Stopping abruptly, I rubbed my eyes, for surely I was seeing things. In the field below were shirtless Highlanders split into groups of two, jabbing, slicing and pirouetting away from each other wielding very large swords. Their long hair whirled out, as did their kilts as their agile half-naked bodies, dipped, ducked, and sidestepped away from their opponents.

Rooted to the ground, I watched my Highlander as his muscles rippled, bunched, and elongated with each movement under a glistening sheen of sweat that covered every inch of his exposed skin as he deftly, swiftly, and accurately wielded his sword, out maneuvering his would be opponent at every turn.

My mouth popped open of its own accord as my body grew heated and my knees became weak. Not able to take my eyes from the surreal scene, I reached down and placed my hand on the rough surface of the rock wall, then sat down before I fell. It was quite a sight to behold and what could only be described as poetry in motion.

At least an hour passed as they continued at a relentless pace until the sun finally slipped down in the horizon and the reddish color of the sky transposed itself into purplish hues turning the full light of the day into twilight.

Before anyone noticed me, I unstuck myself from my gawking spot and went back to the castle to make sure the stew I prepared earlier would be ready for them when they came inside. I only hoped it was edible.

Gavin lowered his sword arm and embraced Morgan with a hearty slap to his back. "That was a fine bit of sparring," he told the brawny man who stood a full head taller than him and who was also the only man older than he was.

"I suppose ye were not so bad either for a mere bairn barely weaned from ye mother's teat."

"Och, Morgan what's this?" he asked jokingly. "More sour grapes ye are spewing from me besting ye once again?"

Morgan grunted and dashed a hand through his shoulder-length white-blonde hair when the wind pushed it forward. "Ye did well enough, I suppose."

"Ye suppose?" Gavin couldn't keep the incredulity from his voice.

"Ye did fine lad." Morgan chuckled then turned and walked across the field to retrieve his dirk he had lost earlier while clashing swords with his Laird.

The rest of the men laughed, all in seemingly good humor after the long bout of training with each other. With the promise of fresh ale, food, and a bath, awaiting them, they made their way off the field and up to the castle.

Gavin watched them go and lifted his arm to wipe the sweat from his brow. Dropping his arm back down, he looked up to the castle and couldn't help but wonder what the lass had gotten into all day while he was training with his men. Knowing her, though, he would not be surprised if she somehow caught the castle on fire even though it was made from stone.

CHAPTER SIXTEEN

Things were a bit different in the castle after the men made their way back inside. They were drinking and laughing with one another, making a good ruckus until they saw me. Then the hall went quiet and wary looks were cut in my direction as I carried out the stew from the kitchen and set it down beside the bowls and spoons on the table.

"Come and get it," I called out as cheerily as I could manage but unfortunately it sounded more like a croaking frog.

Stepping back from the table, I clasped my hands together as one by one chair legs scraped across the floor as the men stood and took turns scooping out ladle's full of stew in each bowl then returned promptly to their seats as all eyes turned on me. What were they waiting for? I cleared my throat.

"Eat, before it gets cold," I told them in a stern motherly voice that I used to get my nieces and nephews to eat.

That seemed to get them going and they dug in with gusto. Letting out a sigh of relief that they were eating, I made my own bowl of stew and walked over to the lone chair in the corner I had occupied the day before for breakfast.

The talking began anew and they at least seemed to be enjoying the meal. If not, they were well-mannered enough not to say anything to me. Well, I amended quickly, that wasn't particularly true. They were saying stuff but I couldn't understand any of it. At least they didn't look green while they were eating this time.

Lifting my spoon, I took a small bite and chewed slowly. Even I had to admit it wasn't too bad considering I was the one who had cooked it. As I swallowed, my eyes drifted to my highlander. It was funny that I called him *my* highlander. Not funny, ha ha mind you, but funny as in strange, since I had only known him for a few short days. As I looked him over, I decided it didn't matter how long I had known him, he was mine, at least temporarily. His long legs were stretched out in front of him as he talked with one of his men, with his hands resting on his taut belly. Reaching forward, he grabbed his drink and his eyes met mine. He gave me a small smile, but the effect it had on me was the same as when I drank too much mead, I felt lightheaded and woozy. In return, I gave him my version of a shy smile.

Unfortunately, it didn't look like it went over to well because his smile turned upside down and slid quickly back into a frown.

I tensed.

How irritating.

Just when I gained an inch, I was pushed back a mile.

After I was finished with the dishes, and cleaning up from dinner, I left the kitchen and walked down the gloomy corridor towards the main hall. Halfway there, I heard a dragging sound behind me. My body tensed and my skin prickled once more as I spun around. But once again, no one was there, at least no one that I could see. Hastening my step, I turned the corner and plowed right into a hard unyielding object.

My breath rushed from my chest as a firm hand closed over my upper arm.

"What are ye doing lass?" he sighed, sounding a mite put out.

"I was …uh…" My mind blanked.

He didn't say a word but his gaze was disturbingly intent as he stared me down.

The moments ticked by and I was very aware of the close proximity of his body to mine. My mind went on a little mini vacation and once again I saw him as he was earlier...swinging his massive sword high above his head as he trained with his men and how his muscles looked glistening with sweat.

"What is wrong with ye, lass?" he asked finally, albeit softly. "Ye look as though ye might faint dead away into my arms."

My eyes traveled up from his mouth back to his eyes and once again the staccato cadence of my heart kicked into high gear. Unsteady on my feet, I swayed into him. His fingers gripped my arm tighter. "I was just..." I gave him one of my practiced sexy looks — the ones I tried in the mirror before I went on dates.

"Lass..." He shook me slightly. "Did ye eat something disagreeable?"

"What?" Mortification set in once again.

"Ye look peaked."

"I'm not sick!"

"Then what's the matter?" he asked sounding genuinely concerned which somehow irritated me.

"I was just..." I started. "Oh, never mind." I jerked my arm away from his grasp.

That look crossed his face again—the pained one and I couldn't help but wonder who was responsible for it. Oh, I knew, I was being a 'b' but the hurt in his eyes had to be from someone else since he barely knew me, which made me even angrier. Not at him, but myself. I always fell for the ones that I could never have.

He turned to leave.

Without thinking I grabbed hold of his arm.

He stopped and looked down at my hand with such intensity I felt like my hand would spontaneously combust. "I'm sorry," I said with meaning.

He exhaled and dragged his free hand over his face. "Nay, I am sorry, lass."

"What for?"

He pulled me roughly against his body. "For this..." His mouth landed on top of mine in a kiss that stole my breath and made my knees weak. I wound my arms around his broad shoulders and slipped my fingers into the ends of his sweat-dampened hair as he pressed me back against the wall. His hand cupped my face as his tongue slipped inside my mouth and lashed against my own. A soft moan escaped my lips.

He suddenly released me.

I grappled for purchase on the wall, my breath coming out in rushed hitches as I looked hungrily up at him.

"Ye keep looking at me like that, lass..." His brow hitched up a notch.

"Like what?" I whispered out barely breathing at this point.

"I may have ta toss ye over my shoulder and take ye back ta my chamber ta let ye have yer fill of me."

Stupidly, I opened my mouth to say *yes, please,* but instead one of my practiced snappy retorts flew from my big mouth before I could stop it. "Yeah, right, as if..."

His body tensed and his eyes narrowed. "Take that haughty tone with me lass, and things will not bode well for ye in the future."

I flinched, not only from his tone but also from the frightening look in his eyes. "I didn't mean it the way it sounded."

A crease pulled his dark brows together.

"I'm just nervous…I guess."

He smirked at me and I was instantly irritated again.

"Come, lass," he said in a commanding tone as though he was calling a dog to him.

"Where are we going?"

"Ta bed."

CHAPTER SEVENTEEN

Through the hall and past the curious stares of the other men, I walked behind him resigning myself to my fate. I would have to sleep with him. *Darn.*

The hinges squeaked as he pulled the door open. Nervously, I followed him inside. A tub was in the middle of the room again and my face immediately flamed imagining what naughty things he had in mind for me tonight.

Standing off to the side, I clasped my shaking hands together awaiting his instructions on what to do. Leaning down, he tossed some wood on the fire and then stood. He didn't look at me though, which seemed strange. He discarded his clothing and climbed into the tub. Once again, I got a good eyeful of his perfectly sculpted buttocks and felt another rush of heat climb to my cheeks.

Letting out a satisfied groan, he leaned his head back against the rim of the tub.

Standing by the door, I kept waiting for him to say something but as the minutes ticked by and still he said nothing, I took a tentative step forward so I could see his face. His eyes were shut.

"What are ye waiting for lass?" He cracked an eye open.

"Oh, oh…" Did he want me in the tub? You can do this Paige, I told myself as I pulled off one of my shoes.

"Lass, what are ye doing?"

"Huh?" I nearly fell over and had to steady myself on the edge of the table. "Well, I was…"

"Come here, I can't see ye from across the room."

"Oh...okay." I hobbled over to the tub with one shoe in my hand.

He looked at the shoe and then up to my face. "What are ye doing with that shoe?"

"I was taking it off?"

"Why?"

"Uh, well...you know..." I lifted my brows up and down.

"Och, lass..." He made a face. "Get on with it, would ye."

Something didn't sound right. His tone wasn't endearing and his expression wasn't the least bit sexy. Bending over, I yanked off my other shoe. Stumbling forward, I nearly fell into the tub but his firm hand grasped my arm, stopping me. "Thanks." I gave him a cheesy grin.

He frowned.

"Alrighty then," I muttered as a flash of heat spread to my cheeks again.

"Lass, have ye been drinking?"

"No." I suddenly wanted to have a drink though. On second thought I might want to have more than one, maybe even two, or three, just to calm my nerves.

Leaning back in the tub, he closed his eyes once more. "Lass," he sighed. "What is taking ye so long?"

So that's how it was going to be. No talk, just action. Taking a calming breath, I undid the buttons on my gown. I made it to the third one...

He opened his eyes and stared right at me with an unreadable expression on his face.

As his eyes drifted down to the front of my gown where my fingers lingered on one of the buttons, I shifted uncomfortably.

"The pitcher is over on the table."

"Oh, right, okay." I walked over to the table, got the pitcher, and walked back to the tub.

"The soap and shampoo are in my trunk." He pulled a chain from around his neck and handed me a key that was attached.

Taking the key from his outstretched hand, I went over to the trunk. Getting down on my knees, I placed the key in the lock.

I unlocked the lid and glancing over at him to make sure his eyes were shut I started to push it upward.

"Don't go looking through my things."

I started from the sound of his voice and dropped the lid.

"I wasn't," I lied. Of course, that is exactly what I was planning on doing. I had been dying to see what he kept inside the trunk since he locked it against me the other night. The lid creaked as I pushed it open again. My eyes landed on a rather large gold foiled box of candies beside the shampoo and soap. There were clothes in there too and many other items that I didn't have time to investigate since I could tell he was watching me. Quickly, I grabbed out the shampoo and soap. Standing once more, I carried them over to the tub.

"The water is getting cold."

"Err… do you want me just to climb in?"

His eyes popped open and his brows rose to his hairline. "What?"

Not the reaction I was expecting. Something felt off. "Uh…what do you want me to do?"

"Lass, are ye sure ye are not daft?"

Irritation flared through me again. "No, I am not daft!"

"Could have fooled me," he muttered.

"That's it!" I stomped my foot.

"Get ta it, lass." He exhaled unfazed by my mini tantrum and wiped his hands over his face, then dropped them back into the water, which made an inviting splashing sound.

Maybe he didn't want to do *it* in the tub, after all. "I need a rag."

"A what?"

"Something to wash you with," I explained.

"There's one in the trunk."

Quickly, I crossed the room, grabbed a rag off the top and resumed my spot at the back of the tub.

"Hair first," he instructed.

"Right." Okay, so maybe he only wanted me to wash him and then he would get to this sleeping business in the bed. That was A-Okay with me. Just like the other night, I got a nice big glob of shampoo in my hands and slammed it down on top of his head. Letting my frustration out, I scrubbed his hair with verve.

He groaned in bliss.

Figures.

CHAPTER EIGHTEEN

Sometimes things don't go as planned. Or so I told myself for the umpteenth time while I tried to get comfortable on the little crappy fur in front of the fire.

After I washed him, he didn't bother getting dressed but merely walked across the room in all his naked glory and climbed into his bed.

Stupidly, I stood there waiting for him to call me to him. But as the minutes ticked by and my feet were getting needles in them from standing still so long, I was beginning to wonder if I had been a bit presumptuous about the evening activities I was sure he had planned for me.

Finally, I heard him let out a lengthy sigh and tensed, sure he was going to tell me to get into bed with him. A shiver of excitement rushed through me as I reached up and fluffed my hair. Blowing on my hand, I checked my breath.

"Lass, what are ye doing?"

"I was, um, waiting for you to tell me what to do," I said trying to sound...sexy.

He let out a derisive sounding laugh.

Apprehension settled between my shoulder blades and I tensed again, not with expectancy but instead with dread.

"Ye want me ta tell ye what ta do?"

I bit my lip hard, knowing somehow nothing good was going to come from me answering him but once again, stupidity reared its ugly head and I stepped right into a pile of steaming crap. "Yes."

A mocking laugh erupted from him. "Yeah, right, as if..." he said, sounding very modern, throwing my words back at me as another mocking laugh erupted from him.

I clenched my fists to the point it hurt, even though I knew on some level I deserved what he said from how I acted earlier.

"Go ta bed, lass," he said finally, albeit quietly.

Feeling like a dog being reprimanded and told to lay down, I did as he said, all the while trying not to cry my eyes out.

Gavin stared up at the ceiling feeling a heavy weight pressing against his chest, crushing against him. He felt terrible for the way he had treated the lass, but what was he to do...beg? Nay, he had been down that long road before and was wary of what he would find at the end. Rejection was not something he cared for, and he would do just about anything to stop it from happening again. So when she had acted so callously toward him, even after he opened his heart to her, he couldn't seem to stop himself. He heard her crying, smothering her tears, and again a piercing pain shot straight past the wall he thought he had built up to protect himself from matters such as this and yet the awful pain had somehow found its way into his heart just the same.

When I woke the following morning he was not in the room. I was starting to wonder if he did it on purpose because no one wanted to eat my 'Oatmeal Surprise' again. Note to self: if you want to get out of doing something for other people make sure you do it badly the first time and then they won't want you to do it anymore.

For some reason it took me longer to get ready than usual. I tried to blame it on lack of sleep but I knew it had more to do with depression than anything else did. It was the strangest thing. I had thought things between us were progressing rather nicely, *until you acted like a 'b'*, my little voice yelled at me. For once, I found I could wholeheartedly agree with my little voice. I was my own worst enemy, a self-saboteur. I was making the same mistakes in the past that I had made time and again, in the future. I was so worried about being hurt that I ruined everything before it even got started.

I was a coward.

I always blamed everyone else for everything that happened or didn't, but maybe I was the cause all along? Because of fear. Fear that I might get hurt. Fear that I might not be good enough. And now that I was actually living a dream come true and got my wish…

Heck, I was in the past with my very own highlander and what had I done? I got all bitchy and pushed him away. As I made my way downstairs, I had an epiphany and I suddenly knew what my problem was…it was quite simple really…I was an idiot.

When I got downstairs, the hall was empty. I knew I should feel relief that I didn't have to cook for the men, but instead a heavy suffocating shroud of depression closed in on me.

Hoping for a pick me up, I thought about going back to his room and breaking out the candies I had seen in his trunk but then I remembered he had the damn key. Stomping down the hall I made my way to the kitchen. The back door stood ajar. I walked over to it, thinking someone accidentally left it open or perhaps the latch didn't catch and the wind pushed it open. When I got to the door, I peaked outside. Slivers of light drifted down through the piney branches of the tree I made my broom from. The dog was digging under it. Closing the door slightly, just in case the dog decided to go on attack mode again, I watched him. He turned towards me and wagged his tail. "Good doggie," I said.

He let out a low, rough sounding bark and began digging in his hole again. Sighing, I turned from the door and looked for something to eat. There were vegetables on the table and a skinned rabbit. Using the water in the bucket on the table, I poured it into the pot and lifting a rag I grabbed the rabbit and dropped it into the pot. Next, I cut up some of the vegetables and dumped them inside as well. After that I hung the pot on the hook over the fire, tossed more wood on the hot coals, and then stood back up. Pressing my hands to my back, I rubbed the soreness gathering there.

"Let me, help ye, lass." A hand pressed to my back.

Startled, I flinched away.

"Och, did I scare ye, lass?"

I turned and my heart broke into a gallop. "No," I lied. "Not at all," I said. "I just didn't hear you."

"Aye," he said, pushing his hand through his greasy black hair. It wasn't Gavin, the one person I wanted to see, but another man. "I came to see if ye needed help with anything."

"Oh, no. Thank you though. I was just finishing up." I grabbed a basket from the table. "I'm about to go get some …uh, things from outside."

"What things might those be?"

"You know, err, pinecones and such." It was a stupid answer but it was the first thing I could think of.

Massaging his close shaven beard, he seemed to contemplate my answer. "Ye use them for cooking do ye?"

"Sure." God, what was I saying? He had to know I was lying.

His eyes narrowed. "If I didn't know better, I would think ye were lying ta me but then I say to myself, Broderick, why would the lass lie ta ye?" He stroked his beard again.

"You're right...I wouldn't do that."

He seemed to ponder my answer. "Come here, lass."

I took a step in the other direction. "I really should get going."

"I said," he repeated. "Come here, lass."

"Gosh. Would you, ah, I forgot..." I ran towards the door, shoved it open and fled outside. I could feel him behind me.

The dog lifted its head.

My step faltered.

"Ye like ta play hard to get do ye?" he asked, coming to stand outside the door.

"What? No. It's just like I said, I have to get stuff and the Laird, you know, he is a stickler for having supper ready on time..."

The man named Broderick took a deliberate step forward just as the dog, my furry nemesis, jumped in front of me and started to growl at him.

He stopped his progression. "Och, get out of here ye mangy dog."

The dog got into a defensive stance just like the night he had come into the hall when it rained. Growling low in his throat, he blocked the man Broderick from coming any closer to me.

Apparently Broderick wasn't in a hurry to get bitten because he stepped back. "I will let ye get back to yer work then," he said. "But never fear lass, I will be around to see ta ye sooner or later." He turned on his heal and fled back into the castle.

I was so relieved; I dropped to my knees.

The dog sidled up to me.

"Thanks doggie." I tentatively reached out my hand so he could smell it and then patted his balding head. "There's my hero. You're a good boy," I said.

Apparently pleased with my praise, he stuck out his tongue and licked my hand affectionately.

Not wanting to go back inside because of the creepy man Broderick, I stayed outside with the dog and picked up some pinecones. Not because I wanted or needed them but just in case he was watching me. The door to the cook room stood ajar. Picking up a hefty stick I made my way back inside with my pinecones, leaving the door open in case I needed to flee again.

Thankfully, there was no one here. I set my basket down, checked on the stew, and then with my stick in hand I walked down the dimly lit corridor to the main hall. Checking to make sure the coast was clear; I bolted through the main room straight to the door.

Jerking the door open, I stepped outside.

The bright light blinded me.

Stopping, I let my eyes adjust, and then quickly headed down the stairs past the tree in the middle of the yard to go watch the men train.

Broderick stepped back from the ramparts and made his way back down stairs through the main hall to the cook room. He crossed over to the table and looked inside the basket sitting on top. It was filled with pinecones. Grunting, he slipped out the back and followed the worn path to the Loch.

CHAPTER NINETEEN

Sitting down on a nice patch of grass in front of the low wall I normally sat on, I gathered little yellow flowers and made a makeshift crown while watching and listening to the men train. It was a comforting sound and the fact that Broderick was not around, made it even better. Although, I did have to wonder where he was — not because I liked him, but the opposite — he scared the shit out of me.

Gavin, in the midst of a heated sparring match with Morgan, looked up and saw his lass sitting on a patch of grass. His attention momentarily diverted, Morgan slammed into him and he fell backward into the dirt.

"Och, Laird, I bested ye." Morgan let out a hearty chuckle making his beard and belly shake with mirth. He held out his hand for his Laird to take.

"Aye, Morgan, ye did," Gavin agreed. He clasped Morgan's hand let him pull him back to his feet.

Dusting off his backside, he looked back to the lass.

Morgan followed his line of vision and grunted.

Gavin turned back to Morgan. "Are ye going ta let me go at ye again, or are ye too tired, old man?"

"Aye, I think I need to take a rest for a bit." Morgan was lying of course but he could tell his Laird had other matters he wanted to attend to.

After Morgan walked away, Gavin made his way over to the lass.

So caught up in what I was doing, I didn't notice Gavin standing in front of me until he spoke.

"Lass," he said. "Care if I sit with ye for a bit?"

I looked up. "No. Of course not." I patted the grass beside me. "I have a very fine seat reserved just for you." I was trying to be nice. Make up for upsetting him earlier.

"Ye do?" He gave my seat I pointed to a doubtful look.

"It's nicer than it looks."

He chuckled. "Is it now?"

"Yes. I'll have you know, it's a very fine seat."

"I suppose I will have to try it ta find out."

"I suppose you will."

He sat down and wiggled his bottom on the grass. "Aye, I think ye are right. It tis a verra fine seat."

Something was fine all right, but it had nothing to do with the seat he had taken. A light sheen of sweat was glistening on his bare chest and his damp hair hung loosely around his very broad shoulders.

A sudden shyness assailed me again. I took the crown of flowers I made and placed them on his head. "Your crown," I said.

"Och, lass, ye are going ta make me look like one of the fairy folk."

I laughed. I couldn't help it.

He frowned. "Ye find me amusing do ye?"

"No. Not you."

Pulling the crown of flowers from his head, he placed them on top of my head instead. "There," he said. "Ye have a more fitting head for a crown, I think."

I tentatively touched the crown on my head.

"Nay lass, leave it be. I like the way it looks on ye."

Blushing, I pulled my hand away.

"I'd like ta see ye *only* wearing that crown of flowers."

My face flamed brighter, catching his meaning, or at least I thought I did. "You, um…would?"

"Aye. After ye scrub the filth from my body," he added with a glint of humor in his eyes.

My toes curled in my shoes and I swallowed hard. I had all I could do not to jump on him right here, right now. He looked so damn sexy. "Is that so," I finally managed.

"Unless ye have something else ye would prefer ta do ta me?" His brow lifted.

"Um..." I chewed on my lip. "What about supper?"

"After supper, then," he said.

"All right," I agreed. "After supper."

"And my bath."

"And your bath," I said.

"Good." He shook his sweat-dampened hair away from his face.

A pregnant pause passed between us. It was a bit awkward to say the least. I didn't know what else to say.

"I should get back to training...unless ye want me ta stay with ye for a wee bit longer."

"No!" I blurted, feeling a bit too warm suddenly. I needed to wash up and ...

His brows creased and for a split second I saw that look of pain enter his eyes again. He stood up abruptly.

"I didn't mean…" I reached out.

He stepped back. "Och, lass," he heaved a sigh, coming to some kind of decision I was not part of. "Not ta worry," he said with a hefty amount of disdain. "I will no force myself upon ye this night or any other for that matter." With that he turned and strode away back to the training field, leaving me all alone.

After supper, I waited for him up in his room but he did not come for his bath or come to bed. Finally, when I couldn't stay awake any longer, I crawled on my crappy bed and fell into a restless slumber.

CHAPTER TWENTY

After my not so wonderful night, I straightened his room. I didn't need to make his bed since he never came to it. And if he did, he left before I awoke.

Bending over, I picked up my ratty fur from the floor, folded it up and set it on the trunk. Walking over to the screen, I was surprised to see that the fresh bowl of water that had magically appeared for me every day was not there. Sighing,

I made myself as presentable as possible. Then I headed down to the kitchen to start some kind of stew to cook for the day and to find myself something to eat. I noticed by the way my gown fit that I was losing weight, which was something that never came easy to me before.

When I rounded the corner, I saw the dog. Instead of running in the other direction, I made my way over to the table and lifted one of the bones I had let dry overnight and tossed it to him. We had come to a truce of sorts after that day with Broderick—a mutual understanding. He stopped growling and trying to eat me alive and in return I gave him a bone to chew on. Most days, Elvis, the name I decided to give the dog hung out with me in the kitchen until I finished making the stew and cleaning up. Then he left me alone to go outside to bury his bone.

Wiping my hands on a towel, I made my way to the back door. The sun was shining and a nice gentle breeze was blowing from the west. I could hear the clashing of metal in the distance and knew the men were training.

We had gotten into a routine of sorts.

The men would fend for themselves for breakfast and then head out to train. They would stay out there until the sun set while I cooked and cleaned for the day. I saved some seeds from some of the fruit and vegetables and decided to go and try to plant them in a little patch of rich dirt out the back door. I wasn't too sure if I was even doing it right, but it gave me something to do with my time besides cleaning and cooking.

I still didn't know the men very well. Callum and Muir were really the only ones that spoke with me, but it was usually just polite conversation about the weather and their training.

Alec and Graham were more standoffish but they did have a ready smile for me and a kind word or two on most days, especially when I washed their plaids.

Morgan was the oldest as far as I could tell. He was quiet and watchful. But not in a creepy way like the man called Broderick. I liked him least of all. He was cordial enough after our encounter that morning in the cook room but he gave me the creeps because he always seemed to be watching me when he thought I wasn't looking. So needless to say, I tended to stay to away from him as much as I could.

The other men weren't as memorable. They seemed nice enough but they kept to themselves mostly. A few days I tried to talk with them but they didn't seem interested in talking to me, so I finally gave up trying.

And as far as *my* highlander was concerned, if possible, he seemed to be getting better looking as the days passed. I would watch him, hoping for one of his rare smiles, or a flirtatious gesture, like he had in the past. My attraction to him grew, but it would seem it was one sided.

After what happened on the training field he pretty much closed himself off against me. And who could blame him? It was my own stupid fault.

Every once in a while I would catch him looking at me, and I would smile, but he would just turn away.

I was beginning to wonder if I blew it with him for good. But luckily for me, I wasn't easily deterred. I had a plan. And it was a good one. In his trunk, he had a deck of cards, and tonight I was going to teach him how to play poker.

Thunder shook the room, as I sat cross-legged on his bed and dealt out the cards. I coerced him to the room under the guise of being afraid of the storm. After one of his staple eye rolls, and an audible sigh, he reluctantly came upstairs with me.

Lighting streaked outside in flashes of bright white light. "Come on," I called over my shoulder cheerily as he tossed another log on the fire.

"Lass, yer a demanding sort are ye not?"

"Oh come on," I said laughing. "You're just afraid I will best you once again."

"Och, not likely," he said in that sexy way of his that made my toes curl and my body heat as he crossed the room, removed his boots, and climbed on the bed.

The firelight cast flickering shadows across the room as we were seated across from one another on the bed. It was like we were in our own little world.

Pulling my hair up away from my face, I twisted it into a loose bun, and picked up my cards.

"What game are we playing?" He lifted his brow at me and my heart did an involuntary flutter.

"Ah, five card draw."

"What's that?"

"Just look at the cards I've dealt you and I will explain as we play." He gave me a curious look. "It's easier this way," I said, wishing we were playing strip poker instead of for the candies he had sitting on the bed.

"All right but don't cheat again."

"I don't cheat."

"Sure ye do."

"I do not." I was getting riled again and then I looked at him. His eyes were alight with laughter and I had all I could do not to throw myself at him. Instead, I rubbed the back of my neck and then undid one of the buttons on my gown. "My, it's a bit warm in here." I fanned myself.

"Not ta me," he answered with a devilish grin.

"Of course," I mumbled dejectedly. Still, I wasn't ready to give up on my attempts at seduction. When he wasn't looking I quickly undid another button on my gown and pressed my arms together so a good amount of my cleavage was showing. I used exaggerated movements to lean forward and pick up my cards.

"Now what?" he asked, seemingly unfazed.

Blowing out a slow stream of air, I deflated my cheeks. "Now you bet."

"Bet?" He lifted his cards up.

"Yes. You put out what you think you should bet against me?"

"But they are all *my* candies."

"I know that!" I snapped getting annoyed, part because he didn't seem to notice my boobs were hanging out and the other part because I wanted some of those candies. I was having withdrawals from lack of sweets and caffeine.

"But what do ye have ta bet with?" His dark brow rose an inch and his lips curled up in that sexy way of his, which immediately made me forget why I had just been so annoyed.

"I can, uh…."

His broad shoulders hunched forward.

"I can give you a massage," I blurted.

"I bet three candies," he said, lifting three of the aforementioned candies from the box wrapped in gold foil. The way he was laying them out with something akin to reverence almost made me laugh and my mouth water at the same time.

"Just three?" I asked skeptically as my eyes drifted with longing at the full box of chocolates.

"Aye, just three," he said.

"Fine," I sighed as that flair of annoyance shot through me again. "Now," I said, lifting the deck. "How many cards do you want?"

"I do not want any."

"You have to *want* at least one."

"Nay, I do not."

"Well, I am taking four." I lifted my Ace of Spades and showed him.

"Why are ye showing me yer cards? Are we done then?"

"No, but to get four cards I have to show you an Ace." I took my four cards off the deck. I had two measly pairs, which consisted of two queens, and a pair of eights.

"Now what?" he asked, looking quite pleased with the hand I dealt him.

"You can bet again or call."

Again, he gave me a curious look. "Call?"

"Yeah, you ask me to show you my cards."

"All right," he said as his lips curved upward into one of his heart-stopping smiles again. "I'll call ye."

"Two pairs, Ace high," I said and laid down my cards. "What do you have?"

"Ye tell me." He shrugged his shoulders and laid down his cards.

I couldn't believe my eyes. He had four Kings and an Ace to boot. "You win," I said grudgingly.

"That was fun."

"Sure it was, since you won," I muttered as I gathered the cards.

"Do I get my massage now?"

"I guess," I told him as I slid the cards back into the little souvenir wooden box with Grandfather Mountain Logo imprinted on the top.

"Good." He loosened his shirt from his kilt, flipped around on the bed, and pillowed his head on top of his arms.

After I set the cards on the trunk, I gathered up my skirts and climbed across the bed to his side. "I should probably get on your back. It would be easier."

"Ye do what ye must," he muttered into his elbow, already sounding half-asleep.

"Alrighty then," I muttered as that familiar flair of annoyance shot through me again. Lifting my skirts, I straddled his waist. Careful not to put my full weight down on him, I rubbed my hands together to warm them and then placed them on his muscled back. His shirt bunched under my hands as I squeezed.

"Och, lass, that feels nice."

Pressing down, I massaged the knots from his shoulders and slid my hands over every hard plane, following the dip in the center of his back to the point where his bottom was curving upward. His shirt was loose and I slid my hands under the fabric as my fingers caressed his warmed skin. It felt like velvet, actually, better than velvet—he had the softest skin I had ever felt, much like a newborn. My fingers slid down farther to the point that the tips were touching the curve of his bottom again and kneaded there. He made a groaning sound and a delicious surge of heat shot between my legs. It was a definite turn on to touch him in such an intimate way. With each stroke, my fingers slid lower and his muscles tensed. Meticulously, I kept up my rigorous massage, and every groan he made gave me another delicious quiver of delight as I pressed down against him all the while wishing he would turn over so I could really press down.

"Should I turn around so ye can massage the front of me as well?" he asked as though he had just read my mind.

"Sure, if you like," I said trying to sound sexy.

"Ye all right, lass?" he asked sounding concerned.

"Yes," I swallowed hard... "Why?" I tried for sexy again.

"Ye sound like ye swallowed a frog."

Oh my ...! "Just a scratch in my throat," I lied baldly.

"If ye say so..." He turned so quickly I was almost dislodged from the top of him. Grabbing my hips, he steadied me and adjusted his hips under me so his erection was situated directly between my thighs. Another burst of heat shot up between my legs. Once I saw his face, I wasn't sure him turning over was such a good idea. It was hard not to stare at him, harder still not to lean forward and kiss those inviting irresistible lips of his.

"Are ye comfortable, lass?"

My eyes met his heavy lidded gaze and I had all I could do to breathe let alone speak.

I nodded instead.

Gently squeezing my hips, he urged me to continue. At least that is what I thought he was trying to tell me. Who knew, but I was going for it.

Leaning forward, I placed my hands on his taut stomach, and pressed my palms down on his six-pack. Each muscle cut perfectly in the flat of his stomach. Granted, I had seen him completely naked in the tub but this was altogether a new experience for me and I decided right then and there it was one of the most erotic things I had ever done with a man.

The firelight danced across his face, shadowing his eyes in the darkness as my fingers climbed up each hill and dipped down into the cut valleys where each muscle was compartmentalized. My body responded, and each time I moved my hands, I dipped down against his erection to the point he was pressed right against me. His fingers kneaded my hips as mine became bolder, climbing up to his chiseled chest and retreating down to the point where his hipbones cut another valley into the warm velvet muscle I was exploring.

Sliding my hands down lower, my fingers followed the slight line of hair that disappeared down underneath his kilt. He removed his hands from my hips as I dipped down against him once again and for a moment, I tensed, thinking he may want me to stop...then he reached up and filled his palms with my breasts and his thumbs slid over my nipples sending an electric surge straight through me. I gasped in pleasure at the same time he groaned.

In an instant, he was sitting up, and I was flush against his erection. One hand went to my back, holding me as he buried his face in my cleavage. The rough scruff of his unshaved face rubbed against me sending another delicious shiver through my body. Before I could think a coherent thought, his tongue slipped in between my breast, making me arch against him more. Then his mouth traveled from one nipple and over to the other, then his lips climbed upward again to my neck. When his mouth found mine, I no longer cared what I was thinking. Nothing mattered except what he was doing to me, this very instant, that we were together.

A low feral growl emitted from deep in his throat as he somehow managed to move me from his lap and onto my back. He came over me, leveraging on his elbows.

"Get comfortable, lass," he instructed.

Feeling shy suddenly, I grabbed hold of one of the furs as I leaned back against the pillows. He sat back on his feet. "Nay, lass," he said, his voice raspy with desire.

Slowly he pulled the fur away.

I backed up as far as I could go.

Giving me a devilish grin he lifted up my gown.

Then he disappeared.

CHAPTER TWENTY-ONE

Twisting the sheets, my head butted up against the top of the bed. He was between my legs, his mouth, his tongue, touching me. Reflexively, I tried to close my legs, but he pressed his hands against my thighs, keeping my legs wide as his tongue flicked against me, repeatedly, bringing me so close to the edge I thought I might just tumble over.

Suddenly he stopped and pulled back out from under my gown. His hair was mussed and he had a slight sheen of my desire on his mouth as he hovered above me. I forced myself not to grab hold of him and bury his face between my legs again.

His lips turned up into a smug smile. "I see ye don't find me so repulsive now, do ye?"

"No." I shook my head. *Wait… who the hell said he was repulsive? Not me…*or did I? For some reason I couldn't remember, but he was anything but. I shook my head again. "Gavin…"

"Laird," he said.

"Laird," I repeated.

A triumphant look crossed his face as he slid his hand slowly up my leg to the wetness between my thighs.

I moaned and squirmed against his hand.

"That is more like it."

My body was on fire, I felt like a bow too tightly strung that I would snap at any given moment.

Gavin wasn't sure what to make of the lass in his bed. Her amber eyes glazed with passion and he knew she wanted him, but she would not tell him. And as much as he hated to admit it to himself, he wanted to hear her say she wanted him. He *needed* her to say it… with words, not just her body and how she responded to him. Even now, he could smell her sweet scent still lingering in his nostrils and her salty taste, still on his tongue.

"Say it, lass…" he prodded.

"What?" I played dumb, not wanting to tip my hand. Whenever I told a man how I felt everything always went downhill from there.

"Tell me, ye want me..." he coaxed.

I was going to put up a fight, not wanting to make the same mistakes I had in the past but then, I just couldn't. What would be the point? Self-deprivation was never my strong suit anyway. All my attempts at dieting had gone to the wayside too. "I do."

"Ye do...what?" His brow lifted.

"For God's sake!" I sighed. "Fine, I want you. Are you happy now?"

"Aye, lass, more than ye will ever know," he said with meaning.

Dipping down, his mouth found hers again and in moments, he had positioned himself outside her wet welcoming warmth. Letting out a feral growl, he captured her mouth at the same time he thrust inside, filling her completely.

On and on, he continued his onslaught, making me writhe and moan. His name on my lips as my fingers dug into his muscular back. He thrust inside of me again. And when I didn't think I could take any more he retreated.

Continuing his rigorous pace, I writhed against him. His hips dipped down, slowing. Clenching his muscled-buttocks he met my hips once more. Not able to help myself, I cried out.

"That's it, lass," he encouraged, reveling in the sweet torture he was eliciting.

She tightened against him. Gavin moaned. He was beyond himself, beyond anything he had ever known, he increased his tempo, pumping harder, faster. Her hands shoved into his hair, pulling and clawing his back. Slicked in sweat he pumped faster, harder, pushing her, pushing himself, until she finally lost all control.

As she shattered against him, she cried out, "I love you."

Gavin met her cries of passion with his own as he too finally slid right over the edge alongside her. Panting and covered in sweat, he smoothed his hand over her sweat-dampened hair and as the last of the tremors faded, the words she had said finally penetrated his brain. They were a spear to his heart, settling deep inside filling him with soul-deep pleasure that he had not known before, even when he was with Jillian. The girl he thought was his one and only... true love.

Leaning forward, he pressed his forehead to hers, staring deeply into her eyes. "Lass, did ye say what I thought ye said?"

I stared up into his blue-green almond shaped eyes and could see what it cost him to ask me that seemingly simple question. Not able to help myself, I nodded enthusiastically. "Yes, my Laird, I do love you."

A slow smile spread across his face. "So, ye finally admit what I've known all along."

"Hey..." I pushed against his sweat-dampened chest. "Watch it or else I may have to take it back."

"Nay, lass ye can not take it back." His face grew serious. "I already have it locked tightly away right in here," he touched his hand to his heart, "and I won't be giving ye back the key."

In that moment, I fell completely, unequivocally, in love with him.

CHAPTER TWENTY-TWO

Gavin stayed awake for sometime after the lass declared her love for him. It warmed his heart. With her head on his shoulder, he smoothed his fingers through her hair, starring up at the darkened ceiling, wondering what he was going to do. He needed a sacrifice when the moon was full again. But how could he do that to her knowing how she felt about him, and also knowing how he felt about her even though he did not utter the words out loud. Deep in his heart he knew the answer. But if he did nothing, surely his men would. Not having any answers readily available, he slowly albeit reluctantly, drifted off into a restless slumber.

The following morning when I woke, I was surprised and a little upset to find I was alone in bed. Rolling over, I hugged his pillow, smelling his heady scent as my mind rehashed the best night of my life.

Being with Gavin was...wow. Really that was the only word I could find that remotely came close to what I had experienced with him. And even though he didn't tell me he loved me too, I convinced myself that he did. Reluctantly, I released his pillow, climbed from bed and got ready for the day. As I walked to the screen, I felt sore but I didn't care. I just had the best sex of my life and a few aches and pains was well worth it. If I had my way, I would be this way every morning.

Later in the day, after I finished my chores, I went down to watch the men train. Sitting in my favorite gawking spot, I watched *my* highlander hack away at his opponent as though he was battling a demon...not one of his men.

I didn't know what to make of it. Shouldn't he be in a good mood? I knew I was.

The longer I watched though, the more unsettled I became. It seemed as though darkness was shrouding everything. Even the skies above had an ominous quality to them.

Once they were finishing training, I slipped away up the well-worn path towards the castle to check on dinner. An abundance of wildflowers dotted the path. I stopped and bent over to pick some for the table.

I gathered a good sized bouquet and stood back up. Pressing my hand to my lower back, I massaged the soreness.

Heavy dark clouds moved across the horizon as day faded into night. Blades of green grass slid over on its side as the wind pushed its way across the rolling fields. Taking a deep breath, I clutched the flowers in my hand and started back up the steep incline. Almost to the top my skin prickled. It was same feeling I got in the castle a few days ago. I felt as though I was being watched. I tried to ignore it, chalking it up to my overactive imagination and kept walking up the path to get supper on the table and start the water boiling for the baths.

I rounded the corner and pulled up short.

Broderick, my least favorite highlander, was leaning against the wall, his massive frame crowding the pathway.

I had a sudden urge to run back the way I came but I squashed it down, and started walking again.

Broderick leered at me as I tried to pass. "What are ye about, *witch*?" he scathed the word.

"I'm not a witch." I tried to step past him.

He scoffed. "I know what ye are." A glimmer of something akin to hate filled his eyes as he blocked my way. "There is no need ta lie ta me."

"I'm not lying to you," I snipped, hoping to put an end to the conversation once and for all. "Now, if you will excuse me, I have chores to attend to." I took another step.

He grabbed my arm roughly and jerked me backward. My flowers scattered down on the path as my body slammed against his, knocking my breath from my lungs.

"Not so fast, lass," he scathed as his fingers cut into my arm.

"What do you want?" I jerked my arm but it did no good. He was holding on too tightly.

"Only the same as our Laird, I want ye ta tell me what ye know about the treasure."

"What treasure?" I had no idea what he was talking about.

"Come now, lass. I can keep a secret. I swear if ye confide in me, I will help ye escape when the time comes."

"Why would I need to escape?" I jerked my arm again, but instead of letting me go he tightened his hold.

He gave me a dubious look. "Ah, he didn't tell ye about the treasure you are supposed to retrieve?"

"No. I know nothing about a treasure." He pulled me closer and his heady scent filled my nostrils, making my stomach churn.

He smiled but it wasn't nice in the least. "So ye don't know."

"I already told you that I don't anything about a treasure," I told him. "Now, could you please let me go, I have supper to prepare."

He loosened his hold and I jerked my arm away.

"Och, what are ye doing?" a male voice sounded from behind.

"Mind yer business, Callum," snapped Broderick.

Callum walked closer. His eyes, the same green blue shade as my highlander, flitted back and forth between Broderick and me. "She is my business. I am supposed to help her get water for our baths."

"Says who?"

"Our Laird, that's who," Callum said pulling himself up to his full height, which was still several inches beneath Broderick and nowhere near his girth.

Broderick leaned down close so Callum couldn't hear. "I'll be watching ye," he said and then stalked off down the path towards the fields.

An eerie sense of dread filled me as I watched his departing form.

"Lass, are ye all right?"

"Yes," I said, rubbing my arm.

"Was he troubling ye?"

"No," I lied. "He was just asking me about supper."

His brows creased with concern. "Are ye sure?"

"Yes. I am sure."

He gave me a doubtful look but didn't press the issue. "Come, lass, I will walk with ye." He extended his arm.

Thankful for the support, I put my arm through his. We walked to back to the castle leaving my lovely bouquet of flowers behind in the dirt.

CHAPTER TWENTY-THREE

After the evening meal, I went back to Gavin's chamber to get his bath ready. I didn't want to stay down in the main hall for longer than necessary because I still had an uneasy feeling from my encounter with Broderick. Thankfully, he didn't come to dinner.

Taking the large cloths off the chair where I had laid them to dry earlier, I placed them across the back of the wooden rim of the tub.

The door creaked open and Gavin stepped into the room.

"Hello," I said as cheerily as I could. He had been so quiet during supper. Granted he was always quiet, but he seemed to have something on his mind. Something that I wasn't sure I wanted to know about.

He undressed without a word, handed me the key to his trunk, and climbed into the tub.

Not knowing what to do, or how to approach what happened to me today, I busied myself by getting the shampoo and soap out of his trunk now that I had the key. I didn't try to look at the contents like I normally would.

"How was training today?" I crossed the room and set the shampoo on the floor.

"It was acceptable."

"That's nice." I dropped the soap in the water.

He slanted an eye open and looked at me.

"What?"

Dipping his hands in the water he lifted them back up and splashed water on his face. Wiping the excess away, he reopened his eyes and gave me a pointed look. "If ye have something to say lass, just spit it out."

It always amazed me at how well he could read me. "Well, I was wondering about something." I slid my fingers through the length of his hair, untangling the silken strands before wetting it down.

"And that would be?"

"Well, I was wondering about…something I heard."

"What did ye hear?" He closed his eyes once again.

I cleared my throat. "I heard there is a treasure."

He tensed. It was subtle and if I wasn't touching him I wouldn't have noticed. "It is just a silly legend, nothing more."

"What kind of legend?" Something about his tone and the way he was acting had my heart jumping into double-time.

"I already told ye, it is of no consequence," he snapped.

I drew back away from him feeling as though he hit me. He didn't of course, but the tone he was using with me made me feel like he had.

Needless to say, after he snapped at me, the conversation I was trying to broach with him about the treasure and Broderick squelched to a halt. The silence was strained and made me feel even more uneasy. I didn't know what was wrong and didn't know what to say to pull him from his obvious funk. He hadn't acted this aloof in a long time. I thought we were past that now, but apparently I was wrong.

After I finished washing him, he got dressed, which wasn't that weird, but then he crossed over to the door and left the room without giving me a second-glance.

The tears that had clogged in my throat while I was bathing him came bubbling to the surface. I sat on the floor and cried, wishing for the first time since I had been here that I was back home. Once my eyes were swollen and all my tears were drained, I stood up and undressed. Laying my clothes over the chair, I crossed the room and climbed in the tub.

Feeling numb, I leaned back, hoping the water would warm the ice in my veins. It warmed me, but did little to dispel my black mood, however. And once I was finished, I was feeling more depressed than ever. Going through the motions, I got ready for bed and then paced the room awaiting his return. I knew I couldn't sleep until he came back into the room. My depression turned to anger and I had half a mind to go search him out and give him a piece of my mind. But then I thought about all the men in the hall and changed my mind.

Tired of pacing, I sat on his bed. Reaching out, I smoothed my hand over one of his many furs on the top, noticing again that they were a lot nicer than the crappy one he had originally given me to sleep on. I clutched his pillow to my chest and inhaled deeply. I could smell his heady scent lingering on the fabric and my heart made another involuntary flutter.

CHAPTER TWENTY- FOUR

Gavin sat in front of the fire in the hall with his legs stretched out in front. He felt terrible about how he treated the lass, but what was he to do? Tell her he made a deal with the witch and in doing so had sealed her fate to die. He couldn't do that. Not now. Not ever. But she wouldn't understand that.

Leaning forward, he poured another drink for himself and then settled back into the chair once again. Gnawing deep down in his belly, guilt was eating him from the inside out. He had only just found the lass, the one that could make him forget and now he would have to let her go. If Jillian hadn't left him of her own accord he would have done the same for her, or so he told himself. It didn't matter anymore, anyway. He could barely remember her face. Instead, another face came to mind when he tried. And she was, at this very moment, upstairs awaiting his return. Damn the King and the treasure, he thought bitterly.

Letting out a lengthy sigh, he scrubbed his hand over his face and then dropped it back to his side. He had made up his mind. Tomorrow, when the moon was full, he would take her to the mist and let her go.

"Where's the lass," Broderick asked, breaking into his dark thoughts.

Gavin looked up. Broderick's face blurred in and out of focus. "Resting."

"She did well with supper this evening," he said, making small talk as he pulled a chair up and sat down.

He gave Broderick a strange look. He didn't remember him being at supper. He shook his head thinking he must have forgotten. "Aye, I suppose she did."

"What will ye do with her?"

He lifted his brow. "What do ye mean?"

"Are ye going to use her ta get the treasure?"

"I haven't given it much thought." He took another drink.

"Aye, I can see yer dilemma." Broderick made a grunting noise which drew Gavin's attention to him once more.

"What are ye getting at?" Gavin blinked, noticing Broderick had a strange gleam in his deep-set eyes.

"Far be it from me ta tell ye how ta handle these types of women …"

"Types of women…?" Shivering in spite of the warmth coming off the fire, Gavin twisted in his seat and lowered his cup before he took another drink.

"Aye, ye know…" Broderick lowered his voice, "the witches."

"She is no witch." His body tensed.

Broderick gave him a doubtful look. "She did come through the mist."

"So what of it, they all do."

"Aye and they are all witches."

"So say ye."

"How can ye deny what we all know?" Broderick gave him a look filled with disdain.

"What ye all know," Gavin snorted, and waved his hand. "What of the men, were they witches' as well?"

"I am guessing so."

"Then where did they go?" Gavin shook his head and immediately regretted it because it made his brain feel funny and his vision blur again. He looked down into his cup. He hadn't had *that* much to drink had he? For some reason he couldn't remember. "Spit it out, Broderick. I grow weary of yer dancing around."

"If we are ta get the treasure, the witch said we must use the girl."

Another shiver of something akin to dread slid up his spine. "Aye, I know what the damn crone said."

"Then when are ye going ta do it?" Broderick prodded.

"When I get damned good and ready, that's when," Gavin snapped.

Broderick reared back, his eyes narrowed and his hands tightened into fists. "Och, ye will get us sent back to the gallows with that kind of talk."

"Laird." Gavin kept his cool but he was ready for him if the need arose, well, he hoped he would be—if the damn floor would stop moving under his feet.

"What?" Broderick glared at him.

"That is Laird ta ye or have ye forgotten?" Gavin leveled him with an icy stare that had brought many a man to heel in his past.

Broderick shook his head and grumbled something unintelligible under his breath. "Nay, I have not forgotten, *Laird*," he scathed the word.

"And ta answer yer question," he poked, "I am Laird here, which means I am the *only* one who will decide the fate of the girl, do ye understand?"

"Aye," Broderick said begrudgingly. "But remember the King awaits his bounty and if ye do not give it ta him like ye said ye would we will all suffer the consequences, not just ye." Broderick turned back towards the fire with a scowl.

Gavin watched him, his drink forgotten. Now he remembered why Broderick was the least favorite of his men. He was too damnable perceptive for his own good.

"Psst, Muir," Callum called softly as he looked warily over at his Laird and then to Broderick, who was his least favorite. There was always something about the man that made his skin prickle when he was around him, so Callum steered clear of him as did most of the other men.

"What are ye whispering for Callum?" Muir covered one of his eyes to stop from seeing double.

"*Shhhhh…*" He lifted his finger and missed his lips.

"What are ye shushing me for?"

"I am trying to eavesdrop," Callum said, as he cupped his ear.

"If yer trying to eavesdrop then why are ye speaking ta me?"

"Cause I can't hear what they are saying?"

"Then how on Earth can ye be eavesdropping if ye cannot hear?"

"I wanted ye ta listen for me?"

"Och, Callum why would I want ta do that?"

"Ta hear what they are saying." He rolled his eyes and then grabbed the table to keep from falling out of his chair. "What are we drinking?"

Muir peered down in his cup with his one eye. "I don't know but it has a hefty kick. A*yeee*," he slurred.

"A*yeee*, ye have that *ri*…ght." Callum slid from his chair under the table.

"Callum, what are ye doing down there?" Muir leaned over to peer down at his friend.

"I'm holding the floor down."

"Callum the floor isn't moving..." Just as he said it, the floor wobbled and he had to steady himself on the table to keep from falling over. "Good work, Callum." He hiccupped and fell backward onto the floor.

"Muir, what are ye doing?" Callum peered over at him from under the table.

"I'm holding down the floor, too."

"Good work," Callum said and then his eyes rolled back in his head as he promptly passed out.

Muir would have agreed but he passed out as well.

Gavin heard another thump and looked over his shoulder. Another one of his men had fallen to the floor. He turned back around. The room blurred. It would seem the only ones still standing, or in his case sitting, was Broderick. Prickles sprung up on his skin. Something wasn't right. He felt it in his gut. Gavin turned his head and the room spun in slow motion. He pressed his palms to his eyes. But it did no good. He still felt like he was moving.

A sickening feeling bubbled up from his stomach. Stumbling from his chair, he swerved around one of his men that passed out on the floor. This was nothing new, his men often slept in the hall when they had too much drink. As he sidestepped around another one of his men, the momentum carried him across the room swiftly. He hit the rough stone of the wall hard but remained standing.

Broderick turned to watch him.

Gavin always had good instincts. And they were telling him he needed to get out of the hall. Bracing himself on the wall, he decided a short lie down wouldn't be such a bad idea. Out of sheer determination, he forced his feet to move. Each time he lifted his foot to move forward he leadenly slammed it back to the ground and repeated the action until he made it to the stairs.

Grabbing the wall, he used it to help him make his way slowly up the stairs. It took all he could do not to fall down.

At some point, I must have dozed off because I was startled awake by a strange dragging sound coming from outside the door. Half-asleep, I stumbled out of the bed. The wood scraped on the stone floor as the door opened.

Wobbly on his feet, Gavin zigzagged across the room and headed straight for his bed, but then he stopped and picked up the folded fur on his trunk.

"L*assss*," he called, slurring.

"Yes." I stepped forward from the shadows.

He turned and gave me a strange look. "Come here." He wavered.

Taking a calming breath, I made my way over to where he stood, thinking he wanted to apologize.

"Here," he shoved the fur into my hands.

"What's this?"

"Yer bed." He took two steps forward and fell face first into his own bed.

Mouth agape, I stood there, feeling so many emotions coursing through me at once I didn't know which one to feel first. As it turned out, one overrode the rest and as I lay down on my filthy bed, I started to cry, again.

A minute later, he started to snore.

CHAPTER TWENTY-FIVE

Not surprisingly, when I woke his bed was empty. With swollen eyes from crying half the night, I got up and splashed water on my face. My heart sank a little more when I realized he didn't even bother bringing me clean water today. Taking my time, I finished washing and then started straightening the room. Gathering up my fur, I rolled it into a tight ball and tossed it on the trunk. A mix of emotions jumbled inside of me. I didn't know what I did wrong. Was he acting so distant because I told him I loved him and he felt bad because he didn't feel the same way? My chest tightened at the thought. Maybe I shouldn't have told him how I felt. And if he didn't do those things to me, those marvelous, wonderful, incredible things to my body, I may have been able to keep my feelings to myself. So, in a way, it was his fault. Not mine.

I grabbed up his pillow to fluff it but punched it hard instead before I tossed them back on the bed. Apparently one of my jumbled emotions finally won out against the rest... anger.

Fired up, I jerked his furs back across the bed and stormed across the room. Jerking the door open, I stomped down the dimly lit corridor, down the stairs and into main hall. I didn't care if the other men were around this time. I was planning on giving Gavin a piece of my mind. I wasn't some....

I pulled up short.

The hall was empty.

But it wasn't like the other mornings when I was left alone. Chairs were overturned and there was an ominous quality to the room. My skin prickled and I rubbed my arms. My anger disintegrated, turning quickly to fear.

Once again I had a feeling I was being watched. I turned slowly around, hoping, no praying, that it was my over active imagination kicking into high gear again but when I turned, someone was there, and that someone was looking right at me.

"Good day to you," I said as cheerily as my shaking voice would allow.

"Och, lass, mayhap it is a good day for someone but not for ye," said the tall wiry man with a smirk. He was not unattractive but there was something sinister lurking in his deep-set fathomless black eyes. Fingers of ice crawled over me and I had an overwhelming urge to run. For once, I didn't second guess myself.

I took off running.

I barely made it across the room to the door when rough hands grabbed me and slammed me back into the table. The edge caught me in my belly and I could scarce catch a breath. I gripped the sides to right myself. A body pressed up behind me and yanked one of my arms off the table as a hand closed over my breast, squeezing the delicate flesh as he jerked against my bottom, trying to lift my gown. My fear turned quickly back to anger. I bucked and kicked, trying to dislodge him, knock him off balance so I could grab the tankard near the edge of the table. I could feel the swell of his erection pressing against my bottom.

"Och, lass. Stay still."

Like hell I will, I thought as my fingers closed around the tankard.

He made a low growling noise as he flipped me around.

Using the momentum to my advantage, I slammed the cup into the side of his head.

He staggered back with a confused look on his face and then lifted his hand to his head. Pulling his fingers back down, he stared at the blood dripping down from the tips. "Why ye little bitch," he snarled and took a step forward.

I threw the cup as hard as I could.

It hit him square between his eyes. This time when he staggered backward, he kept going and collapsed to the floor.

Shaking all over, I stepped over his body. Running across the room, I yanked open the door and was instantly blinded by the sunlight. Stumbling, blind, I made my way down the stairs to the courtyard, bracing myself under a tree, trying to get my vision back. Something creaked over my head. I looked up. Hanging above me from the tree was a foot, and then another. Caught in the middle of dangling feet, I screamed.

CHAPTER TWENTY-SIX

A fist slammed into Gavin's belly, waking him. Two men that he didn't recognize yanked harder on the leather strips binding his wrists. The burning taste of bile slid up his throat as the dinner he had eaten only hours before regurgitated out from his mouth onto the ground beneath his feet.

"Not so haughty now, are ye, *Laird*," Broderick scathed.

"If only ye would let me loose I would gladly show ye how haughty I can be," he mocked in a deadly tone, as another blow landed on him from behind into his kidney. This time the metallic taste of copper filled his mouth from his own blood.

"I see ye still have not learned yer lesson," Broderick clasped his aching hand.

"What lesson might that be?" Gavin taunted as another meaty fist slammed into his chest and a rib made a sickening cracking sound from the impact. Instantly, he heaved, fighting to bring air back into his lungs.

"Just tell me where the lass is and ye can go back with yer men, where ye belong."

Gavin fought to keep his eyes open, although doing so gave him an unholy view of dangling feet that belonged to his men, some who had only just become old enough to be called such. And he had failed them. He failed them all, including the lass.

"Not ta worry, I will find her," Broderick boasted.

"I'd wish ye luck in that but I would prefer ye went back ta hell."

Broderick's face twisted as he flexed his fingers. "When I find her, and I will," he promised. "We will see if the lass can do what the other failed to do." A sneer broke across his face.

His words brought Gavin back from his slipping consciousness. "What are ye talking about? Jillian left of her own accord, she went back…"

"She sunk she did, like a rock," Broderick jeered. "Well," he amended chuckling. "She did once we weighted her skirts down with rocks."

"Ye killed her?" Gavin felt ice pour through his veins, freezing him from the inside out. She didn't leave him like he thought.

"I think that is too harsh a word." Broderick rubbed his knuckles. "Ye see…she couldn't swim with the extra weight, so she drowned." He shrugged his shoulders indifferently.

"Why ye sorry excuse for a …." Gavin fought against the restraints with renewed vigor.

"Watch the name calling, *Laird*," he scathed. "I only did what ye didn't have the guts ta do yerself."

She didn't leave him after all. A bone crushing sadness closed in on him and he could barely take a breath. "She was innocent."

"Och," Broderick snorted. "She was a witch, just like the one that's here now." He took a step forward and lowered his voice, leaning down close to his face. "Although I have to say she was a mite comelier than her replacement, aye?"

Rage tore through Gavin. Jerking forward, he freed one arm and slammed his fist into Broderick's smug smiling face.

Stumbling back from the blow, Broderick clasp his eye that was already swelling shut. Letting out an earsplitting roar he charged forward and slammed his fist into Gavin's jaw.

Gavin's head snapped back like a whip from the impact. When the darkness came for him this time, he went willingly.

Hidden in the bushes where I dumped the rushes, I stayed hidden and listened to the exchange between Gavin and Broderick. I couldn't see the tree with the dead men, which I was glad for. The feet dangling above my head would be forever burned into my memory. Biting back the urge to be sick, a familiar ache settled upon my chest, not only for the men but because of what I just heard. Gavin knew about the so-called treasure all along. And he was going to sacrifice me. To what, though? I still didn't know, but whatever it was, it couldn't be good. And if that wasn't bad enough, now I knew why Gavin acted the way he did towards me. He was in love with another. And Broderick killed her, just like he was planning on doing to me if he found me.

Someone walked by.

I didn't dare turn or move a muscle. My hiding place was not the best. If someone looked over the side of the stairs they would surely see me. But it was the only place I could find on short notice.

A blustery wind kicked up a good amount of dirt and debris. The tree limbs creaked in protest bringing the unholy sight of the men I had seen hanging from the branches back.

My stomach lurched. Bile burned its way up my throat and into my mouth. Terrified, I would be heard, I forced it back down.

It seemed like hours passed but it could have been only minutes. Time didn't have much meaning when a person was trapped. The men finally left the courtyard and made their way into the castle. I hunkered down under the dirty rushes, barely breathing.

It was already growing dark. Ominous clouds swirled above in the gray sky. Against the eerie backdrop, Gavin hung limply from one of the low hanging branches, with his arms stretched above his head. He wasn't moving and his head was cocked strangely to the side. I didn't know if he was alive or dead. I tried not to think about it.

Making sure no one was about, I peered through the branches. I could hear the men inside the castle, laughing and making a good amount of ruckus. I cringed from the sound. How could anyone laugh and carry on like that when such horror was right outside the door. "Monsters."

Trying to be as quiet as possible, I crawled out of my hiding place and came nose to nose with Elvis. He wagged his tail happily and then slobbered a good amount of spit on my face when he licked me with his tongue.

Rubbing his balding head, I pushed him back and stood up. "Stay," I told him in a low voice so I wouldn't be heard. Thankfully, for once he listened.

Gathering my skirts in my hands, I crouched down and sprinted over to the tree. The door was open and there was a straight view to where I was. I ducked around the side. Hoping against hope they wouldn't look outside, I crossed over to Gavin. He looked so white. Blood dripped down the side of his face and my stomach lurched in protest. "Please don't be dead," I prayed as I lifted my hand to his neck. I could feel his pulse — thank God!

Standing on my tip-toes, I reached up to unbind the leather strips on his wrists. The limb creaked and bobbed under his weight.

I nearly got him untied.

His body jerked against mine and knocked me off balance. I fell backward against the tree. A dangling foot was just above my head. Stifling the urge to scream, I looked back at the castle to make sure I was still undetected. Thank the Lord they didn't seem to see me.

"Gavin, it's me," I whispered as I made my way back to him. His eyes looked crazed, frantically searching for where my voice was coming from. I tentatively reached out and placed my ice-cold hand on his heated skin. He flinched. "It's all right," I lied. Nothing was all right.

"Lass?" He shuddered out a breath of air.

"Shh, don't waste your breath. I'll have you untied in just a minute."

"Ye have to run, run as fast as ye can," he was talking quickly.

"Not without you." I finished untying his wrists.

His full weight fell down on me and I had all I could do to keep standing. I shouldered him upward and slung his arm around my neck. "Can you walk?"

"Aye, I think."

"You have to do better than that. Come on," I used my sternest voice hoping it would spur him to move faster.

"I thought ye were dead," he rasped, sounding surprised I wasn't.

A surge of annoyance shot through me. "Well, I'm not, so come on." I jerked him and he immediately gasped in pain. I felt bad but we didn't have time to dawdle, or make small talk.

"Aye, I can see ye are not dead," he griped, and took another long shuddering breath.

"If you don't get your ass moving we will be," I snapped. My anger was dwindling fast and fear was creeping back out to grab hold of me, and if that happened, we'd both be screwed.

CHAPTER TWENTY-SEVEN

Lass, listen ta me," I heard Gavin say with urgency, which didn't seem right. My head listed to the side, trying to get away from the insistent tapping against my face.

I opened my eyes to the darkness and immediately screamed.

A hand promptly covered my mouth, quieting me.

"Shh, lass, do not scream," he warned.

"Gavin?"

"Aye lass, it's me," he said softly.

I got my bearings and the horror of what I had seen came rushing back. "All those men...they're dead..." A fresh wave of tears slipped from my eyes as the cloying feeling I had felt earlier came back to take hold of me.

"I know, lass." His voice carried the weight of a great pain and sadness as he spoke.

"Why?" It was the only word I could manage.

"They want the treasure."

"The treasure..."

"Aye, the treasure," he repeated.

"I thought you said there wasn't a treasure."

"I lied."

"Why?" A sickening feeling settled in my stomach as I remembered a bit too clearly what finding the treasure entailed. I scooted away from him.

"What is wrong?"

He sounded so concerned, I almost caved. "You lied to me."

"I didn't have much choice."

"You didn't have much choice..." I sounded like I was a broken record.

"Aye."

"You had a choice. You just chose not to tell me." I stood up and stepped into water. The frigidness of it made me gasp.

Gavin didn't move. "I know. I lied. But I didn't know....I didn't know..." he repeated, quieter now.

"What didn't you know?" I sloshed my way through the water back over to the ledge I was on moments before and climbed on top.

"I made a deal."

"What deal?"

"With the witch," he mumbled.

All my fear went to the wayside again. "What witch?"

"The one that sent you here," he said and I could hear the strain in his voice. I wasn't sure if it was because he was upset or in pain.

"What about her?"

"The King is superstitious. He thinks witches are making his boats sink and stealing his gold."

"What does that have to do with anything?"

"Everything. Don't ye see?"

"No. Gavin. I don't' see."

"I was...am, supposed to retrieve it for him in return for my freedom."

"So what is the problem? Why don't you get it for him?"

"I would but there is a wee problem."

"What is this wee problem? Surely you..."

"It is protected by the monster," he added quietly.

"There's a monster? There's no such thing." Even as I said it, I had a hard time swallowing it because there was no such thing as traveling to the past, and yet, here I was.

"Aye, lass," he said, seemingly knowing I had just come to that very same far-reaching conclusion.

"What do I have to do with this...monster?"

"I was supposed ta sacrifice ye ta it."

"What the hell are you talking about?" I pushed farther back up on the rocks.

"Lass, stop fretting, I was not going ta do it."

"Then what's wrong?"

"Other people want the treasure and they will stop at nothing to get it."

"So let them take it."

"It's not that simple."

"I still don't get what that has to do with me?"

"Everything, lass," he said so quietly it was only a whisper of air.

"Wait? What? I don't understand." A rush of water slid inside the cave and lapped against the rock I was standing on.

"Lass ye made a deal with a witch ta come here."

"I did not!" I was adamant. "It was that damn Gypsy or...wait...are they the same?"

"Aye, lass," he sighed. "Did she draw yer blood?"

"Well, yes. I already told you that."

"Then ye made a binding deal, then."

"I did?"

"Aye, lass, ye did."

"So this is my fault? All the men…it's my fault?" I had a hard time standing. I felt like my legs were going to buckle under me.

"Nay, lass," he soothed. "Broderick would have found another reason to do what he did. I think he is trying to take the gold for himself and in doing so, double cross the King."

"Are all of the men…?"

"Not all, but most," he said answering the rest of my unspoken question.

My heart constricted with heaviness. "Why?"

"They were in the way."

"I don't understand," I told him and I didn't.

"Lass, there is no time."

"But if I didn't come here…if I didn't make the deal with the Gypsy…"

"Nay, lass." He shifted to the side. "It still would have happened sooner or later. If it was not ye than it would have been someone else."

"Like it did to…" I almost told him what I heard earlier about the girl he loved, but my heart constricted, making it hard to catch a breath, let alone keep speaking.

"I know lass," he sighed. "She tricked us all."

"Did the…" I swallowed hard, "the witch, kill all those men?"

"Nay, not the witch." I felt him shake his head.

"Who then?"

"It was that bloody bastard, Broderick."

Icy fingers of dread crawled over my skin. Just hearing his name made me feel sick. "But how could one man get so many of the others?"

"He must have drugged the ale. It was easy after that. The poor bastards didn't even see it coming."

Even though I couldn't see him, I could feel his body grow rigid. "How did he get you?"

"I heard the commotion as I was heading downstairs…I saw what was happening, I tried to escape…"

"You just let him…" I couldn't finish. It was too horrible to consider.

"Lass," his voice was hoarse as he spoke. "Sometimes ye need ta make hard choices in life that are not the best, but sometimes, it is better ta try ta run so ye may fight another day than ta stay ta fight and die in vain."

"Is that what you did?"

"Aye, I tried but didn't make it very far."

"Laird…" I said, out of habit, still trying to come to terms with what he was telling me.

"Gavin," he said.

"What?"

"Call me, Gavin, for I am not worthy of that title any longer."

"Yes, you are," I argued, feeling his pain.

"Nay, lass, a laird protects his men, he doesn't let them…."

"It's not your fault," I cut him off before he could say the rest.

"Aye, it is," he admitted. There he had said it out loud and even though he had damned himself and his men, he still felt a bit of tension ease from his chest from the admittance.

"Why are you saying that?" My voice hitched in my throat.

"It does not excuse my actions, or lack thereof."

"You had to, you said so," I argued, feeling desperate." I felt as though I was freezing from the inside out. I couldn't breathe right; I couldn't even think straight. "Stop, please," I begged.

"Listen ta me." He grabbed my arms and shook me slightly. "Ye have ta listen ta me."

"I *am* listening to you."

"When I tell ye ta run, run as fast and as far as ye can. Stay hidden until the mist comes and then slip inside of it and ye can get home."

"Home…"

"Aye, lass…" he said. "The moon will be full soon, and the mist will come as it always does," he tried to explain. "Ye must get inside of it, let it take ye when it pulls, do not be afraid."

"But you'll be with me, right?

Silence that stretched between us, which was all the affirmation I needed. He wasn't coming with me.

"Nay, lass, I can not go," he finally said.

"Why?" I struggled to find the right words to make him see reason. "It's too late for them…" Even though I knew it was true, saying it out loud made me sick to my stomach. "But…not you," I finished on a sob.

"It is too late for me as well. I was damned a long time ago. I have only been walking in a shadow of my former self, biding my time until this day came."

My mind spun. I was trying to figure a way out of this mess but my brain wasn't cooperating. Fear for him…for me…was muddling my thoughts.

I pushed it down. Trying to stay strong…be brave…but I was none of those things. I was a coward—always had been. Didn't I just admit that to myself a short while ago? Was it because of the other girl, his love, the one he lost I couldn't help wondering in some sick part of my mind. Was that why he didn't want to come with me?

Icy fingers of dread wound its way around me. At my bleakest point, I didn't see a way out and I was suffocating with it. And just when all my hope had all but shriveled up inside of me another voice cut through the murkiness, the hopelessness of it all…

A glimmer of what *could be* wrapped itself around me and brought with it a calming realization that I could do this...for him, for her, for the men who died in vain, for us all. I had to.

"Och, lass," he breathed, lifting his hand to my face and cupping it gently, taking my silence as something altogether different, acceptance maybe? "I enjoyed our time together," he said valiantly and I was sure if I could see his face he would be trying to give me one of his sexy heart-stopping smiles to make me feel better.

A sudden rush of emotions tore through me. Anger, thank God, won out. "How stupid are you?"

His body tensed and he dropped his hand. "What did ye just say ta me?"

"Oh, so now you'll just what? Sacrifice yourself for them? They are already gone. If you stay to avenge them you will surely die."

"Aye, mayhap but it would be for something worthy."

"What could be more worthy than your own life?" I argued, feeling desperate.

"Lass, ye are," he said softly, reaching up to lay his hand on my face.

I grabbed hold of his hand. "No." I shook my head. "I won't let you."

"Ye do not have much choice in the matter."

"I got you into this mess and I'm not going anywhere without you."

"Shh, lass," he sighed, caressing my face with his thumb. "We don't have much time."

Face to face, eye to eye...we stared at one another in the darkness. I reached up to his face, feeling the hard angles of his jaw, his thick lashes, the sweeping curve of his brows, his nose, his lips... "I love you."

"Aye, I know," he breathed.

Holding my face in his hands, he leaned down and touched his lips to mine. The kiss was painstakingly sweet...a good bye kiss.

CHAPTER TWENTY-EIGHT

A flickering torch light was headed toward the entrance of the cave.

Gavin jerked away from me and pushed me behind him. "They are coming."

"Who?" I was still reeling from his kiss.

"Och, lass, the men who want ye to die."

"What?" I couldn't believe it. Or rather, I didn't want to believe it.

"Listen to me, lass," Gavin said quickly. "I will create a diversion. When I do, ye need to run. Run like the hounds of hell are chasing ye." He grabbed my arms and dragged me down into the water with him.

I gasped.

The water felt like ice.

"Lass." He shook me and my head rattled on my shoulders as water lapped higher on my legs, nearly touching my thighs.

"I don't want to go out there.

"Och, lass, I know. But we don't have much choice in the matter. If we stay we will drown. I think we should take our chances with the men. Mayhap I can talk some sense into Shamus if he's out there. He isn't a bad man, just desperate."

"That doesn't sound very reassuring to me," I told him. Desperate people make bad choices all the time. So what was stopping him from making another bad choice and feeding me to some monster? He didn't know me, and he certainly didn't owe me anything. To him I was just another witch — even though I wasn't. But how did one go about making someone from the past see that?

"It will be all right." Gavin took my freezing fingers into his own, squeezing them reassuringly.

Muir and Callum climbed quickly over the rock-laden beach to the front of the cave along with Graham and Alec. They had barely escaped death. It was coming for them, or so Callum had thought when he woke to the God awful noise of branches creaking in the early hours of the morning. Feeling sick from too much drink he had went to the door to relieve himself, and that is when he spotted the men...the ones he didn't know, throwing ropes over the branches of the tree. Luckily he had the wherewithal to pull Muir, as heavy as he was, off into a small room in the back. Head pounding, he went back for Graham and then Alec, but after that, it was too risky to get the other men. Staying in the shadows he waited for them to wake, holding his sword at the ready, while witnessing the foul deed Broderick was doing to the other men.

Och, he held his stomach. He was sure he going to be sick watching. Somehow he had kept his food down. Broderick, the rotten traitor, pulled the last of the men from the hall; Callum then quickly roused Muir, Alec, and Graham. They were unsteady on their feet but Callum had spurred them along with dire warnings of what was to come if they didn't move their arse's a little faster.

"Muir, why is it so dark in here?" Callum asked, stumbling over the rocks blocking the entrance.

"Because it *is* dark."

"I know it is dark," Callum interjected. "Think ye would be a wee bit kinder since I saved your arse not too long ago."

"Och, Callum, why do ye keep reminding me." Muir clutched his stomach. Whatever drug Broderick had given them was working its way through his innards.

"Muir, stop bickering with Callum and get on with it," Alec said in a harsh whisper.

"See Muir," Callum said. "At least Alec is grateful to me."

"I didn't say I wasn't grateful…"

"Ye didn't say ye were…"

"For the love of God, just be quiet," Graham commanded.

"But…"

"He told ye to be quiet, Callum," Muir added his two cents.

"Och, Muir, ye were talking as well," Callum complained.

"Both of ye shut yer mouths before someone hears ye." Alec pushed past them, holding the torch aloft inside the cave.

"Laird," he called into the darkness.

CHAPTER TWENTY-NINE

Thank the blessed Saints above, they are alive!" Gavin made the sign of the cross over his chest.

I did too, just to be on the safe side.

Grabbing my hand, Gavin pulled me along through the rising tide towards the entrance where the men were waiting.

Once outside, Gavin stood off to my left, saying a few words to his men. I couldn't hear due to the howling wind. Bending over, I pulled off both of my shoes, shook the sand and debris that had gathered inside onto the ground. Shoving my shoes back on, I stood up again and that is when I noticed the four men running up the steep rocky incline that surrounded the cave and then disappeared over the other side. "Where are they going?" I asked when Gavin stepped up beside me once more.

"Ta see what we are up against and try to find some more weapons." He slid the sword Callum gave him into the side of his belt and then shoved a short-handled knife down into his boot from Muir... the only weapons they had.

"Shouldn't we be going with them?"

"Nay. We would only slow them down." He lied. He didn't bother telling the lass the truth that he was sending his remaining men on a fool's errand knowing full well they wouldn't be back in time. But that was fine by him. At least this way he could save four of his men, something he had failed to do with the others. He thought about Morgan and his stomach twisted. He had failed his friend and he would never forgive himself.

"I would not..." I started but then thought about how wet my clothing was and how he was right. "Well," I said. "I get why I might slow them down," I admitted. "But what about you?" I shivered as the wind picked up more strength and pushed against us.

He gave me a curious look. "Lass, I took quite a beating from Broderick and his men." That was true enough, he thought, taking a shuddering breath.

"Laird..."

"Och, lass, I told ye not ta call me that," he snapped. A pained expression crossed his face.

"Gavin, then," I said, quickly, feeling terrible once again. I couldn't even begin to imagine how he felt. Knowing what happened to his men. "What are we going to do?"

He stared off into the distance, and I could tell by the resolute expression on his handsome face that my time here was running short.

In the cave, Gavin told me of the mist and that he wanted me to leave. To go back home, where I belonged, he had said.

But what if I didn't want to go home now? What if I wanted to stay? Sure, it hadn't turned out to be the vacation I thought it would be, but there were definite perks to this timeframe too. There was no competition to speak of. At home, women were in abundance and it was hard enough to get a man and harder still, to keep them. I had learned that hard lesson many times over.

So needless to say, being here, where I was pretty much the only woman to speak of, I was rather enjoying the attention, not to mention the other perks of being in the past. Sure I missed, sweatpants, movies and food, but on a whole this wasn't so bad.

And now I had to leave because of some stupid treasure that probably didn't even exist. The men hanging from the tree pushed into my thoughts and I pushed them right back out. I couldn't think of them right now or I would surely lose what little self-control I still had.

And even though I was putting up a brave front, I couldn't stop myself from trembling. As I looked over at Gavin, I couldn't help but notice how calm he seemed. It was not a good sign. It was as though he had resigned himself to his fate before the battle had even begun.

"See lass, the moon is full, just as I knew it would be." He reached out and wrapped his arm securely around my shoulders.

The full moon he spoke of was shining down on his face, illuminating his resolute expression with an eerie glow. I pressed my head against his shoulder as I tried to recall every time he had held me in his arms, every time he had kissed me, every time he laughed and how his eyes would alight. No matter how far I traveled, I didn't think I would ever be able to forget him.

A deep sadness settled on me, squeezing against my chest and once again I had a hard time taking the slightest bit of air into my lungs.

Wrapping my arms more securely around his waist...I waited for the inevitable to come.

Gavin didn't move much and I couldn't help but wonder if he was in more pain then he let on. His expression was resolute as he stared off across the glassy surface of the Loch as the mist slowly crept closer.

Lifting his hand, he smoothed it over my hair and then kissed the top of my head. I snuggled deeper into his arms, coming to a decision. If the mist came for me, I was going to make sure he went with me. Now all I had to do was figure out how.

"Gavin..." He looked down at me.

"You know I love you, right?"

"Aye, I can see that you do." His expression did not change but his body tensed against mine. A slow churn started in my belly, twisting, and clenching, waiting for him to say something back to me, but he stayed silent.

Gavin knew he should say something. Tell her he loved her too but he couldn't bring himself to it. Not now at least. His mind chided him, if *not now than when*? He knew he may not get another opportunity but found himself not able to say the words aloud he had sworn he would never say to another, ever again. The problem, as it always was, in matters such as this, his heart had other ideas and he found he may have to break the promise he made so long ago to another. As he looked down into the face of the woman who had become his friend, and then his lover, he realized that even though he did indeed love her, he may have to let her go, except even as he thought it, he didn't want to. He didn't think he could, so instead of saying anything, he leaned down and pressed his lips to hers for what would surely be the last time.

The kiss he gave her was meant to be gentle, sweet... a reminder of how he felt about her, to tell her without words. But he found that wasn't enough. His kiss became more insistent. It was deeper, more urgent. He held onto her as though she was his lifeline, using all the pent up emotion he was feeling.

As I kissed him back, I had an awful feeling he was not kissing me because he was overcome with love for me as I was for him, but instead because this would be the last time.

CHAPTER THIRTY

A darkened shadow slid over us and I knew our time had finally run out.

Gavin spun around so swiftly, I almost toppled to the ground. The sound of metal being unsheathed rang out in the air with chilling clarity.

"Lad, drop yer weapon," a burly man called from the top of the hill.

"Get Muir's dirk," he said over his shoulder.

"What?"

"Lass, the knife in my boot," he said.

"Oh." I reached down and pulled out his knife. Standing back up, I pressed myself against his back. "Who is that?"

"A backstabbing, greedy wretch," he scathed. Using his body, he blocked me against the men lined up on the hilltop. "Och, Shamus what have ye done?"

"Sorry lad, but ye know I need the coin for my family."

"But at what cost?" he asked.

"Drop yer sword," Broderick yelled.

Gavin tensed and tightened his hold on his sword. Ignoring Broderick, he lifted his arm. "Shamus, it does not have ta be this way."

More men stepped forward, making a semicircle. It was the two of us against them all.

There was nothing behind us but a body of water and the frigid wind pushing against our backs as though it was trying to make us fall prey to their attempts at butchering us for the monster tucked down deep inside the waters of the Loch.

Although, if truth were to be told, no one had yet to lay eyes on such a beast and I doubted at this juncture that we, or they, ever would. So why we or more accurately put, me, should be sacrificed for this ever elusive and what I considered to be an imaginary beast, was still beyond reason to me. But here we stood nonetheless, with a mere dirk in my hand and a broadsword in Gavin's as he stood to defend me from my execution, or what I preferred to call it, my untimely demise, against the rest.

We would surely die, or at the very least, I would die, and for what? A treasure no one had ever laid eyes on that was hidden in a cave who knew where, with a creature that only had a thirst for young maidens, namely me, which I highly doubted would be the case.

I mean, come on.

Why in the world would the monster be interested in eating me?

Maybe, I could see being a decent candidate when I first arrived, I was plumper, but I had lost a good bit of weight since then. Now I was far from being a filling meal. Certainly that fat man standing to the left of me that was a good head taller and much broader... surely he would be the better choice for the aforementioned creature/monster of the Loch to munch on. I said as much to Gavin, "Why don't they feed that guy over there to the damn monster?"

Gavin cut his eyes in my direction, and then over to the man. "He is not a maiden."

"Well, if you want to get technical about it, neither am I. You saw to that yourself," I whispered hotly. Of course, that wasn't altogether true either since I was far from being a maiden, in the pure sense (as in virginal) long before I even came to this time but I opted not to mention that particular detail.

"Aye, I did see to that, many times," he admonished proudly.

"Yes, you did," I readily agreed and even though this was not the time nor the place, my body heated involuntarily at the thought of being with him, wrapped in his strong arms as he made love to me. Not once, or twice, but three times, in one night.

"Lass, pay attention," he instructed, angling his body in front of mine.

My mind came back from yet another stirring recollection, which was too soon if you asked me. I mean, come on. If I was going to go, I at least wanted to be thinking of something pleasurable when it happened.

"Shamus, the lass is no longer a virgin," Gavin called over the din.

"The monster won't know."

That did it.

"If the monster doesn't know if I'm a virgin, why in the hell don't you feed it the old tubby over there, in my stead?" I yelled, pointing a shaking finger at the aforementioned tubby man.

All eyes turned in the direction of the man I offered up.

"She makes a good argument, Shamus," one of the men in the front said.

The man in question slunk back a few steps when he realized all eyes had turned on him.

"Lass, what are ye doing?" Gavin asked.

"I'm instilling a reasonable doubt."

"This is no trial, lass."

"Isn't it?" I asked. "It sure seems that way to me."

"They do not care, lass."

If the truth were to be told, I didn't either. I only wanted to get them thinking, confuse them, or at the very least draw their attention from us and in this instance I had remarkably accomplished my feat. None of the men were actually looking at us any longer. The mist that Gavin said would come, the one that could take me back to my time, was in fact, at this very instant, heading right for us, gaining momentum from the wind pushing it toward us from the Loch. Reaching over, I grabbed the back of Gavin's shirt and tugged.

"Lass, what?" he said over his shoulder, sounding annoyed which immediately irked me.

I angled my head and motioned behind us toward the water with a tilt of my chin.

Gavin's eyes widened as he finally caught my meaning. Well, at least I hoped he did. I tightened my fingers around his shirt, about to pull him with me into the frigid water and swim to the mist if the need arose.

Although, if possible, I would prefer to take a pass on getting in the water again since I still remembered how cold it was. And if we did not get to the mist quickly we would surely die of hyperthermia before we even reached it. And I would rather not chance that.

An eerie sloshing noise cut through the din of the men, accompanied by a bubbling, gurgling sound. Every head that had been turned in the other direction were instantly riveted on us, once again. I had somehow missed my opportunity to save us. I blew it. Stupid. Stupid. Stupid, Paige, I berated myself.

"Lass," Gavin, whispered hotly.

"For God's sake," I snapped annoyed my pity-party was cut short. "What?"

"Do not make any hasty movements," he warned in a breath of air that immediately sent shivers of dread cascading down my spine.

The old tubby-two ton, I was offering up to be sacrificed only minutes before actually took off up the rock-laden incline moving much faster than I would have given him credit for. My mind finally registered what Gavin had said and all the men's reactions in front of me only added credence to it.

Slowly, I turned, and looked up into the glowing eyes of the infamous monster of the Loch Morar, looming above us.

"Holy *shhh...*"

Gavin wrapped his arms around me. "Do not look."

It was too late for that. I had already seen the God awful looking creature and now I couldn't turn away. Its scaly snake like head listed to the side, and then swung back in the other direction, tracking the movement of the men running.

Like a whip cracking, the head snapped out above us, snatching three men in one fell swoop.

"See, I told you the monster wouldn't care what it ate," I told him, feeling like I was watching a movie, not actually about to be devoured by the monster I was commentating on like some kind of critic. Part in terror and part in astonishment, I watched as the monster made quick work of the three men. A pair of feet dangled out from under the sharp teeth and then disappeared down into its long scaly throat.

Just as the gypsy/witch/legend said, submerged in the water, I could see the glimmering golden mouth of a cave behind the creature, which looked to be filled with a Kings treasure. Hell, if you asked me, it looked like Fort Knox.

Gavin pulled me closer, and pressed my head against his shoulder protectively with his free hand. Instinctively, I wrapped my arms around his waist and hugged him back.

"I will miss ye, lass," he whispered hotly in my ear as his hand stroked down over my back.

Reality came crashing in, smashing my dreamlike trance to smithereens. Trying to force back the tears that were suddenly clouding my vision, I tightened my grip.

"Take heed," he whispered. "The mist is almost here."

I held him tighter. I didn't want to leave yet...maybe not ever...fine, maybe that was a stretch considering what we were facing but I certainly didn't want to leave like this. I had only just started getting used to...all this...and now...I didn't want to go back through the mist. I wanted to stay here, with him, forever.

My legs grew weak. I fought the darkness trying to lay claim to me as the mist came closer. "No. I can't leave you."

"Ye have to." He smoothed his hands over my hair to hold my face in his hands. The monster seemed not to see us, only the men running as it snatched two more into its mouth.

No, I don't, but I didn't tell him that.

He lifted my hand and pressed it with his to where my heart resided in my chest. "I will always be right here with ye."

He dropped my hand and took a step away from me as the mist wound its way around my body, pulling.

"Do not be afraid, lass." A look of pain entered his eyes once more.

"Gavin, what are you doing?" I planted my feet, trying to lean away from the pull of the mist.

"I have to get the treasure while the beast is occupied."

Like hell you will, I thought. The gypsy's words that I had forgotten came back to me in a rush.

"If ye want ta have a Highlander for yer verra own, do ye think ye could keep him from choosing a Kings treasure over ye?"

I remembered with perfect clarity saying, *"Of course I can."*

"I hope ye are right, lass." She patted my bottom and ushered me from her tent. The sound of men screaming brought my mind back to the moment at hand.

"What about me?" I couldn't help asking.

Gavin turned back around and grabbed hold of her arms. "Ye stay put. Do not move a muscle. The mist will take ye away any moment now. Remember what I told ye, aye?" And with that, he turned and dove into the water.

Frozen in place, I couldn't quite grasp what happened. What about his declarations of love for me? Fine. It wasn't the best time but seriously? He wasn't going to see me again. Did our time together mean so little? A deep sadness closed in on me, making it hard to take a breath. Tears came rushing to the surface. I couldn't believe he didn't even tell me he was going to miss me.

I stared at the break of water where he dove, looking for him. Maybe he would wave or call to me from the water and tell me what I so desperately wanted to hear.

When Gavin reemerged from the water, he was already waist deep. He didn't turn around like I was hoping. Instead, he was like a madman, using deep strokes to glide across the water towards the treasure.

I was still in denial. I couldn't quite grasp the fact that he had just left me standing here with a monster making meals out the men running away. And yet, Gavin, my highlander, didn't seem to care. He had chosen the damnable treasure over me.

Well, I had news for him. I wasn't going to give up...not now. Forcing my feet forward, I stepped into the water to follow him.

Treading water, Gavin's head bobbed up and down on the crest of a wave. He was hoping to have one last glimpse of his lass before she disappeared from his life forever. It saddened him greatly, more so then he imagined it would. But it was for the best. If she was gone he wouldn't have to worry about her any longer. He also wouldn't get to see her smiling face anymore or have her shapely body press up against his while they slept or ….

He spotted her, and what he saw made his heart seize. "Lass, what are ye doing?"

"It's all right," I told him, stepping further into the water. "Don't worry about me. Go ahead, get your *treasure*." The word left a bad taste in my mouth. I tried to move forward but it was harder to move now, the mist was surrounding me and like he said it would, I could feel it starting to pull me.

"I told ye ta stay put!" his voice was harsh

I acted like I didn't hear him.

Gavin dove under the water as the serpentine head of the monster swung towards him.

I ducked down too, but the water was retreating so I couldn't go under.

He resurfaced and swiped the wetness from his eyes. "Lass, do not move, not an inch, do ye ken what I am saying ta ye?" The sound of his voice cut me to the bone, and I immediately started second-guessing my hasty decision to follow him.

The monster's head whipped in the other direction as more men made a break for it.

I kept crouched down, trying to cover my face against the smell of death that permeated the air.

A shoe dropped into the water in front of me with a big splash. Belatedly, I realized a leg was still attached. The dream like trance I was in vanished and everything became a very harsh, a very scary reality. I wasn't in a movie. I was in the past with a God awful creature that was apparently really hungry and if I wasn't careful, I too, would be part of its meal. A bubble of hysterical laughter threatened to erupt from me, thinking that I couldn't make this shit up if I tried.

When Gavin saw Paige crouching in the water with the monster so close to her, something snapped. Getting the treasure was upmost in his mind until this very moment. And then he realized something that had been buried deep inside. He didn't really give a damn about the treasure or the King's wrath. What he cared about, the only thing he cared about was getting to the woman who somehow managed to wheedle her way into his heart.

Diving back into the swell of water, the treasure forgotten, he tried to get back to her. He had to get to her, to tell her the truth, before it was too late.

Everything seemed to slow down. And I was sure my short life would flash before my eyes at any moment. But it didn't. Instead, through the mist surrounding me, I saw Gavin. He let out a bloodcurdling roar and just like on the training field, like poetry in motion, I watched, spellbound as he whirled around, with his sword high above his head, slicing it through the air as the glinting metal landed deeply into the scaly flesh of the monster.

Blood rained down onto the water, coating me and everything else in the general vicinity.

Frozen in terror, the most unholy sound I had ever heard surrounded me.

Belatedly, I realized it was not coming from Gavin, the monster, or the men...it was coming from me.

A loud hiss rent the air as the serpentine head swung back around, the glowing eyes settling on me as it prepared to strike.

I couldn't move if I tried. The pull of the mist was too strong.

Gavin let out a feral roar and slammed into me.

Air forced from my lungs from impact as I was plunged deep under the frigid water with him on top of me. Reflexively, I wrapped my arms around his waist. We resurfaced. "Lass, let me go." He pushed my arms.

I was being pulled in two directions. Part with Gavin, and part by the mist.

Instead of letting him go, like I knew he wanted, I did what any sensible woman would have done in my predicament. I tightened my hold and pulled him back through the mist with me.

EPILOGUE

GRANDFATHER MOUNTAIN,
NORTH CAROLINA, PRESENT DAY

The screaming is what woke him when the darkness finally receded from his mind. Gavin pulled himself up into a sitting position and looked around the desolate landscape of the mountain.

It seemed different.

People were milling about, which wouldn't be all that strange, but they were wearing some peculiar looking clothing.

Something shifted beside him and he looked down. The lass, was curled up at his side, still clutching to his plaid.

"Lass…" He shook her arm.

A voice cut through the din I was hearing in my mind. The Scottish brogue unmistakable even with my eyes closed. The fog receded from my brain as my eyes opened. Directly above me was *my* highlander. I sat up and immediately noticed all the people in normal clothing, walking around us giving us strange looks. "We made it!" I threw my arms around him.

His hands clenched my waist, holding me aloft. "Aye, lass, it would seem so."

Little bells of warning were sounding in my brain but I was too happy to worry about them now. "We made it!" I repeated. I hugged him tighter, ignoring how rigid he was.

"Aye, lass, we did," he agreed.

Leaning back, I looked at him. "That was close, right?"

"Aye." He nodded.

"I didn't think we would get out of there. I had my doubts about that mist you told me about…" I was speaking fast not able to help myself.

"Lass," he exhaled. "If ye want me ta respond ta ye, ye need ta speak more plainly."

"Oh, right. Sorry."

"I know what ye did."

"Huh?" I played dumb.

"You disobeyed me." He gave me a stern look.

"Well, you didn't leave me much choice."

A resolute expression crossed his face. "Aye, I suppose you are right about that."

"Are you upset?" I couldn't tell.

"No. I am not upset."

"Are you glad?"

"What do you think?"He gave me another one of his unreadable looks.

"Well…" I hedged. "I hope you are."

He turned and looked across the horizon, then back to me. His expression was grim. "Lass," he exhaled. "What I mean to say is…"

My heart kicked into double time. "It's all right." I waved my hand. "I'm sure this is a lot to take. Well, not for me, but you. You know we are in the future, right?" I asked, speaking slowly so he would understand.

A crease marred his otherwise perfect brow. "I know where we are, lass."

"Of course you do…"

He took my hands in his. "Lass," he said looking deeply into my eyes. "I have something I need to tell ye."

This was it. He was going to finally tell me of his love for me. It was a surreal moment to be sure. I held my breath and prepared myself. However, the longer he looked at me, with those blue green eyes of his, the same color of Loch Morar. The happiness I expected to pour over me didn't come. Instead, a sinking feeling settled in the pit of my stomach. Something was very off.

Not that we were both in the future but something else... "What's wrong?"

"I wanted to..." he trailed off, looking nervous suddenly.

"Oh, who cares," I cut him off. "We're safe that is all that matters. Right?"

"Of course."

Ignoring the warning bells sounding in my mind, I squeezed his hands. "I'm sorry about the treasure." Fine. That was an outright lie. I wasn't sorry about that at all.

"It's all right."

"But you were so close..." I tried to read his expression, hoping he wasn't upset but also trying to assuage my guilt at the same time.

"I know."

"Are you upset I brought you with me?"

"Nay." He shook his head solemnly back and forth. "It was bound to happen sooner or later."

I frowned at him. That didn't sound very convincing. I turned away from him not wanting him to see the tears that threatened to spill from my eyes. He looked the same. But he wasn't acting the same.

"Don't ye know how I feel about ye by now, lass?" he asked, sounding like he was getting choked up.

"Well," I hedged, biting back my tears, not sure if I should admit my worst fear. "Not really." I turned back towards him.

His brow creased more as he stared down at me with those beautiful eyes of his. "I was going to tell ye… I wanted to tell ye…"

The sinking feeling was back in my stomach. "Tell me…what?"

He took a deep breath. The pained look I had seen so many times before made another appearance.

My heart jumped into double time. It didn't look like he was about to declare his love for me. It actually looked like he was going to tell me something that I didn't want to hear. Freaking out, I jumped up. "Gosh, I'm starving…"

In that moment, Gavin made up his mind. Some things were better left unsaid, at least for now. Besides, he had other things to attend to, like finding a certain Gypsy. He stood up and winced.

"Are you all right?"

"Aye. Just hungry."

I didn't believe him but I didn't want to open a can of worms either. At least not now. Not while we were still on this damnable mountain. I would have plenty of time to talk to him about what was bothering him, later, or at least that is what I told myself. "Well, we should get going before it gets dark." I brushed off my skirts acting like I wasn't upset and held out my hand for him to take.

"Aye," he said. "We should go before it gets dark." As he took her hand, Gavin could swear someone was watching them…waiting…

He had been in the past long enough to know his gut wasn't usually wrong. As they headed down the mountain, he could swear he heard the cackling laughter of the Gypsy…Morag.

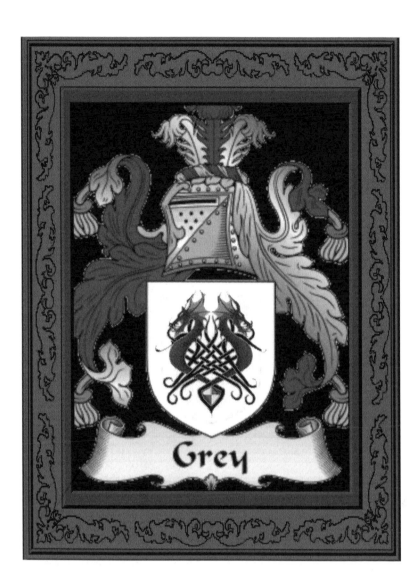

Grey

Be on the lookout for the 'Lost in the Highlands', the Thirteen Scotsman, book two …

<u>TAKE A SNEAK PEEK NOW</u>

Lost in the Highlands, the Thirteen Scotsman, Book Two © by Lorraine Beaumont

"Och, lass," he whispered in a hot murmur against my ear. "What ye do ta me." Gripping my hips, he rocked back on the chair with my legs straddling him. He was rigid, his body slicked with sweat pressed against mine, buried deep within my womb, filling me completely.

"I can't…" I gasped on the verge of the precipice he was pushing me towards.

"Ye can." His hands moved slowly upward from my hips to my breasts, cupping them ever so gently as he lowered his mouth. The rasp of his beard scraped against my sensitive flesh, making me arc like a bow. "When we go, we should go together, aye?"

"I can't," I argued, although the point was moot. He controlled my every movement. "Yes," I finally agreed, clinging to his broad shoulders.

"Aye, that's more like it," he boasted, feeling the threads of his own release bubbling to the surface like molten lava waiting to escape an erupting volcano.

His mouth closed over my nipple. I couldn't take it. Ignoring his command, I purposefully shifted and impaled myself further.

He let out a feral groan. "Och, lass, I told ye ta wait."

Too bad, I thought. Lifting myself, I slowly eased upward. I was the one in control now and I reveled in it. Leaning forward, I nipped at his neck, his shoulder, tasting the saltiness on his skin as I lowered back down again.

"That's it, lass," he breathed, fondling my breasts as they jiggled in his hands. His hips jerked upward against me.

I gasped from the pressure building and then it was too much, I couldn't wait. Losing all control, my body became taut, and then shattered in a million wonderful pieces.

Gavin groaned and flipped her over on her back. Pumping harder, faster, he too finally found the release that they had both painstakingly sought from one another.

Later that night, with the lass snuggled beside him, in a bed far too soft for his liking, he stared up at the darkened ceiling, like he had many a night in the past. He still had found no trace of the damnable Gypsy, Morag. Each lead they found led them to another dead end.

He had yet to tell the lass why he was looking for the Gypsy, Morag. And as far as he was concerned, she didn't need to know...which is what he told himself repeatedly when his guilt began gnawing deep in his belly.

Once the Highland Games returned to the mountain and he found that witch, he would be returning back to his own time. He had to for the sake of his men, for the treasure he owed a King and for the love he had lost so long ago. Yes, Gavin had it all figured out.

Or so he told himself…

Rolling onto his side, he closed his eyes, enjoying the creature comforts this time provided as well as his time with the lass… his lass, for a wee bit longer.

Prepare to get lost all over again...
Lost in the Highlands, The Thirteen
Scotsman, Now Available

A SCOTTISH TIME TRAVEL ROMANCE

Lost
in the
HIGHLANDS
THE THIRTEEN SCOTSMAN

LORRAINE BEAUMONT

RAVENHURST

LORRAINE BEAUMONT

RAVENHURST SERIES

"Fans of Outlander will fall in love with this series filled with swoon worthy knights and unexpected twists and turns!" Romancingthereader

Ravenhurst - A New Adult Time Travel Romance Series.

Begin your adventure through time in this captivating world filled with debauchery, steamy sex, lies, betrayal, and murder. Document the contents of a vast estate, discover riches beyond your wildest dreams, figure out a centuries old legend and fall into the arms of a handsome egotistical Earl, a dashing Duke, an irresistible Wastrel, a mouthwatering Millionaire and ultimately land in the bed of A Knight in Shining Armor.

A once forgotten legend...

Katherine Nicole Jamison never imagined when she took a job at a prestigious auction house for the summer, that one moment of impulsiveness could change her life forever. When she "borrows" an ancient amulet, she inadvertently sets in motion a series of events, which results in her waking up in 18th century England, betrothed to an arrogant, self-centered Earl.

Sebastian de Winter ~ the Earl of Ravenhurst is a renowned womanizer who always prided himself as being a ladies man, until he is left standing at the altar. His betrothed Marguerite vanishes and as if by magic reappears months later. But is she his betrothed?

Ravenhurst ~ locked somewhere within the gloomy confines of this ancient edifice is the key that will unlock the door of time itself.

"What Mystery Will You Unlock?"
TRY OUT THE FIRST BOOK FOR FREE

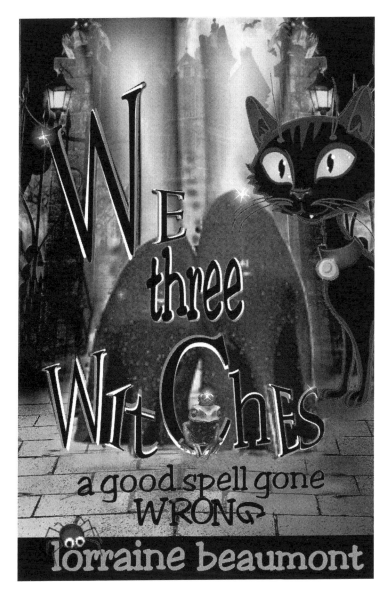

WE three WitChes

a good spell gone WRONG

lorraine beaumont

EDENBROOKE HOLLOW SERIES

A Bewitching Interactive Paranormal Time Travel Romance-

Combine a Supernatural Town, Backfiring Spells, Witches, Mortals, Vampires and a few too many Zombies and what do you get?

A Recipe for disaster.

Welcome to Edenbrooke Hollow

Novice witch *Melody Granger* is on a mission to not only learn the spells she needs to get into the elite circle within her coven but also get the guy of her dreams with one. But when she inadvertently buys a defective spell book from a Charlatan at the local Potions, Broomsticks, and Beyond and her spells start to backfire she realizes that someone may not only be trying to derail her carefully laid plans to join the elite circle within her coven but also get rid of her for good.

Derrick St. Claire -A Vampire with an insatiable appetite... striking good looks and too much money to spend in his many lifetimes wants his ancestral home back from the Black Hat Society's Patronesses who have taken it over for their coven and yearly witches' ball. As far as he is concerned, like oil and water, Witches and Vampires don't mix, but when he encounters Melody Granger a novice witch with a penchant for getting herself into trouble he realizes that some rules, even his own, are made to be broken.

Interactive Game Inside

www.edenbrookehollowseries.blogspot.com

WOULD YOU RISK EVERYTHING TO SAVE A MONTSTER?

LORRAINE BEAUMONT

CHECK OUT LORRAINE'S YOUNG ADULT
SERIES FOR ADULTS
BRIARCLIFF SERIES

"The paranormal romance that centers the story and pulls you into its embrace like a lover you had forgotten how much you enjoyed kissing. There is mystery and more than anything there is the need to find out what dark secret lies at the core of it all. A paranormal romance for those who are not afraid of the dark"
Sookie Stackhouse Reviews

Briarcliff Township may look like any other town snuggled deep within the forests of the New England coastline but it harbors a dark secret. When the winds change, old stirrings arise from forgotten misdeeds and a thirst for vengeance. Something wicked this way comes...
TRY IT FREE!
www.briarcliffseries.blogspot.com

ABOUT LORRAINE

Lorraine Beaumont is a #1 International and #1 Bestselling author and an award-winning poet. Even though she writes is several genres' all of her books are written with an ensemble cast of characters, filled with plenty twists and turns that will keep you guessing until the very end. She has four series to date and is in the process of working on another series.

She lives in Maryland and is currently working on her next novel. For more information, connect with her online:

FACEBOOK / TWITTER / BLOG / PINTEREST / INSTAGRAM

Thank you for reading my book and I hope you enjoyed getting lost in the Highlands with me!

"Life is not measured by how many breaths we take but rather in the moments that take our breath away!"
www.lorrainebeaumont.blogspot.com

If you enjoyed this book please help others enjoy it by spreading the word. Tell others why you liked this book by leaving a review.
If you write a review, send an email to lbeaumontbooks@gmail.com, so
Lorraine can thank you with a personal note.

Made in the USA
Middletown, DE
29 August 2017